THE
BOYFRIEND
BRACKET

THE

BOYFRIEND

BRACKET

KATE EVANGELISTA

SQUARE
FISH

New York

SQUARE FISH

An imprint of Macmillan Publishing Group, LLC
175 Fifth Avenue, New York, NY 10010
fiercereads.com
swoonreads.com

THE BOYFRIEND BRACKET. Copyright © 2018 by Kate Evangelista.
All rights reserved. Printed in the United States of America.

Square Fish and the Square Fish logo are trademarks of Macmillan and
are used by Swoon Reads under license from Macmillan.

Our books may be purchased in bulk for promotional, educational,
or business use. Please contact your local bookseller or the
Macmillan Corporate and Premium Sales Department at (800) 221-7945
ext. 5442 or by email at MacmillanSpecialMarkets@macmillan.com.

Library of Congress Control Number: 2017957583
ISBN 978-1-250-30917-4 (paperback) / ISBN 978-1-250-18539-6 (ebook)

Originally published in the United States by Swoon Reads
First Square Fish edition, 2019
Book designed by Liz Dresner
Square Fish logo designed by Filomena Tuosto

10 9 8 7 6 5 4 3 2 1

To the Grade 11 girls of my
Creative Writing Fiction class of SY 2016–2017.
Your talent and enthusiasm brought new life into my
writing. All of you will run the world one day.

PROLOGUE
GRADUATION DAY

ig brothers suck, Stella thought as she pouted, scowled, and crossed her arms all throughout the ceremony. Not even the California sun and the scent of fresh-cut grass made a difference to her current mood. She should have been ecstatic that Camron James Patterson, spawn of Satan sent to make her life a living hell, was graduating high school that day. Instead the seat reserved for her boyfriend of officially one week remained empty. The guy was a total no-show.

Stella had been extra careful too. She made sure Darryl liked her enough before introducing him to her mom. They had been dating a few weeks prior to the meet. But when Cam found out, he went all guard dog on Darryl's ass. First, it was the probing questions like "What are your plans for my sister?" and "Are you sure you're good enough for her?" and Stella's personal favorite, "What kind of future do you think you have with her?"

No one wanted to think about those things at freaking seventeen! She didn't even think about those things. Ugh! She hated her brother with the passion of a thousand suns.

As if the questions weren't enough, Cam laid the intimidation on thick. How he made sure Darryl knew he slept with his favorite Louisville Slugger close by. How he wasn't afraid to teach Darryl a lesson on manners. And worst of all, the line "Whatever you do to my sister, I will happily do to you," said with a straight face and capped off with a smile. It did the trick, judging from the unanswered texts, tweets, DMs, even a Snapchat SOS. Darryl was officially ghosting her.

"I can't wait until you're gone," she mumbled to herself as her brother climbed the stage and received the rolled-up piece of paper that stood in for the actual diploma. She winced immediately after speaking. The elastics her orthodontist had put in the other day did their job. At least Dr. Africa hadn't run out of the pink ones this time. Stella loved that his last name was a continent.

Rubbing her cheek to ease some of the tightness in her jaw—from the constant gritting of her teeth—Stella consoled herself with the thought that, like her brother, the braces would be gone soon. There would be more boyfriends in her future. With what she had planned over the summer break, there would definitely be more boyfriends. Stella practically rubbed her hands together at the prospect of her impending freedom.

After the ceremony, Stella raised her mom's phone. Watching her fuss over Cam through the screen while she waited for them to pose for the traditional graduate-between-parents photo—minus her dad—she saw pieces of herself. In her mother were her straight, black hair, complexion, and full lips. What her father—may his soul rest in peace—had blessed her with were high cheekbones and a lanky figure. Oh, what she would give for her mother's curves.

Cam was the total opposite. He got their father's light skin, only now it was tanned from all those hours spent under the sun playing baseball. He also got Dad's curly mop and the smattering of freckles across the bridge of his nose. From Mom, he'd received his hazel eyes. Stella wanted those eyes. Luck of the draw in the genetics pool! She was convinced, had she been born first, those eyes would have been hers instead of the plain brown she walked around with. Alas.

"Say cheese," Stella said once they finally posed, and Cam hammed it up, puffing his chest out. She had already suffered through the family group shots. She estimated about ten more photos and her mom would be satisfied.

"Now one with you and your *kuya*," her mom said, using the Filipino term for brother. She waved her hands enthusiastically for the phone while pulling her heels out of the grass every time they sank into the ground as she approached Stella.

"Ugh!" Stella rolled her eyes. "Do I have to?"

"Come on, little sis," Cam said, a big smile on his face, waving her over. "One for the road."

Stella weighed the pros and cons of refusing. She was still so mad at him for driving another one away. Darryl could have been The One, for all she knew. Yet Cam was still her brother. He had his good points. Like the time he'd helped her save a kitten stuck in a tree. Almost broke his arm in the process. Like the time he'd stayed up all night sewing sequins on a dress she wanted to wear for spring fling. Dateless, but still. And that time he'd driven all night before her birthday just to pick up a part for her sewing machine after it had broken down. She was never going to admit it to anyone, but she was going to miss him.

"Stella Marie Patterson," her mom said. Using her full name always meant she had been or was about to be in some sort of trouble.

"All right!" She added a pinch of indignation to her tone.

Her mother nudged her forward.

Stella dropped her hands to her sides and trudged the rest of the way to her still-smiling brother. Once she was at his side, he swung his arm over her shoulders and pulled her closer. Grudgingly, Stella didn't resist.

"Take off your glasses, Stella," her mother said from behind the phone.

Unwilling to prolong the agony, Stella removed her thick, black frames, folding the sides carefully and dropping them into her purse. Then she pushed her braids over her shoulders and smiled—braces and all.

"Happy?" Stella asked through her teeth.

"I'm always happy," Cam replied through the side of his mouth as their mom fidgeted with the camera settings.

Stella lost her smile. "When are you leaving again?"

"Another one bites the dust," Cam sang smugly.

"You're ruining my life!"

"He wasn't good for you."

"In your eyes, no one is." Stella's fingers curled into fists at her sides.

"Trust me."

"How do you even know?" she challenged, glaring up at him.

Cam gave her a sidelong glance. "You hid him. That's all the proof I need."

"I only did that because I knew you'd drive him away. Which is exactly what happened after I finally had the guts to tell Mom. And news flash, *she* was cool with it!"

"Say cheese," their mother said.

Cam smiled. Stella did not.

"Oh, Stella," her mom said with a cluck of disappointment.

Stella didn't care. She was too angry. She pushed away from Cam and faced him.

"I'm tired of you policing my life!" she said, not bothering to use her inside voice. The new elastics be damned. "You hover over me more than Mom does. You're such a jerk!"

"Stella, don't talk like that to your brother," their mother interjected. Her fiery temper was another thing Stella had inherited.

"Stella, I'm only—"

"I'm sick of it," she snapped, cutting Cam off. "Congratulations on graduating. I'm going home!" She turned on her heel, the skirt of the dress she had made swishing with the movement, and stomped away.

"But we're having lunch—"

"Just let her cool off," she heard Cam telling their mother.

Stella kept walking, her kitten heels digging into the grass. She mashed her lips together to keep from crying out of sheer frustration. She didn't even care that everything ahead of her was a blur. All she wanted was to keep moving. Only one thing would make everything better.

"Slappy?" said a rich male voice she would have recognized in a crowded airport.

Flutters woke in her stomach. Even if she hated the nickname he had given her, hearing it never failed to make her knees turn to jelly. She closed her eyes and took a deep breath. Then she pulled her glasses from her purse and pushed them up the bridge of her nose. Only then did she allow herself to face him.

Her cheeks grew hot. Of course she needed to wear her glasses. Why would she want to miss seeing every detail of the perfection in front of her? She liked to think there was a shine of mischief just for her in those brilliant eyes—gray as a sleet sky. The sunlight played in his spun-silk chestnut hair. The strands were tamed for the occasion. The bump on his nose was from a time he fell face-first while skateboarding. The scar on his chin, running parallel to his lower lip, was from the back of Cam's head making contact while they were wrestling as kids. The imperfections gave his looks character. She loved him all

6

the more for them. But his best feature was his smile. All her insides went gooey when he smiled.

"Oh, hi, Will," she said. William Montgomery. Even his name was perfect. The only thing she hated about him was he happened to be her brother's best friend. "Congratulations on graduating."

"Thanks." He bent his considerable height and stared straight into her eyes. She loved that his height made her feel petite even though she was all of five ten. "What's wrong?"

She was torn. On the one hand, she was happy to see him. On the other, she was annoyed. He wasn't innocent in all this. She reminded herself not to be distracted by his perfection. And just like that, her annoyance took over her happiness. She could actually feel it in the coming together of her eyebrows.

"Ugh! *You*." She stabbed a finger at him. "You're just as bad as he is."

"Whoa!" He raised his hands as if her finger were loaded. "What'd I do?"

"More like what you and your 'bro' did." She sandwiched the word *bro* with air quotes.

"Hey! Don't knock the bro code. What'd Cam do now?"

She narrowed her eyes. "Don't deny you had anything to do with it. You're Robin to his Batman when it comes to scaring my boyfriends away."

He shrugged one shoulder and muttered, "More like Sam to his Dean, but whatever. To-may-to, to-mah-to."

"Ugh!" Stella's fists trembled at her sides. "I'm so glad to be rid of both of you!"

Yet where had she heard that boys pretended to be mean to

the girls they liked? Did Will's helping her brother scare away boyfriends mean he secretly liked her? Her stomach flipped. No. She ran a hand down one braid. Will couldn't like her. She knew his type. Tall. Leggy. Usually with straight, blond hair. Stella was none of those things. Stella was braces and glasses and braids.

"That Darryl guy is a huge jerk anyway," Will said matter-of-factly.

Stella whipped her head up, her jaw dropping. Then she pressed her lips together before she said, "Of course you'd say that. For all I know, Cam's brainwashed you into thinking that."

"You know he's only protecting you, right?" He tugged at one of her braids. The gesture never failed to make Stella self-conscious. "And my brain is my own, thank you very much."

"It's killing my social life." It wasn't like she could have the guy she really wanted. That part she left out.

Once, she'd had this crazy notion that she was the Barbie to Will's Ken. Of course, loving Will was just a pipe dream. He was totally off-limits. Cam would blow a gasket. Plus Will didn't see her that way. She was forever in the baby-sister zone. But still . . . being with him would be so worth it.

"Hey, will you do me a favor?"

Will's voice shocked her out of a potentially dangerous daydream involving finding out just how soft his lips were.

"Um . . ." Stella nudged her glasses farther up her nose. "Sure."

What else was she supposed to say? Seriously. Anything for Will.

"I know it's asking a lot. . . ." He paused.

"What is it?" She leaned closer and batted her eyelashes.

"With me moving out, Nana is going to be all alone," he finally said. "Will you check on her from time to time over the summer? Just to see if she's okay? I've got that workshop to attend so I'm leaving earlier than anticipated."

Nana was what Will called his grandmother. With his parents in Doctors Without Borders, he'd grown up with her. Actually, they all had—playing in her huge backyard. She always had a fresh batch of cookies and lemonade waiting for them afterward.

"Of course," Stella said, her heart warming. "You don't even need to ask twice."

Will breathed like a weight had been lifted off his shoulders. He pulled Stella into a tight hug. The shock of the contact was short. She slipped her arms into his graduation gown and wrapped them around his lean waist. Of its own accord, her head rested against his strong shoulder. She inhaled the pre-summer air mixed with his aftershave. Sharp. Spicy. She could smell him all day. For as long as he held her, she would let herself imagine the possibility of them. She could almost taste it. Feel it at her fingertips.

The moment was broken by the bane of her existence because that was just her luck. This was her life. Great. So not.

Cam said, "Yo, bro! We got to go!"

As if her body were a live wire, Will jumped back. Like, literally, jumped away from her. All the elation caused by the hug drained away. She was a bucket with a hole. It was back to admiring Will from afar. Her normal.

9

Will chuckled nervously when he said, "Yeah. Lots to do."

"We were just about to head out for lunch," her mother said. "Want to join us, William?"

Stella wished he'd say yes, but she knew better.

Will gave her mom the sweetest grin. It made Stella's heart dance. "Lunch with Nana. But I'll catch you at the party later?" he asked Cam.

"See ya," Cam said.

Her brother and his best friend shook hands, and that turned into a back-slapping hug. And there she was blushing as if she weren't seventeen and ready to take over Oak Hills High the second her brother was gone. She blamed it on the power of the Will factor. Get her within a meter of him, and her mind went kaput.

Even as her mother steered her toward the car, with Cam leading the way, Stella's eyes followed Will until the crowd swallowed him up as if he were Poseidon returning to the sea. She really needed to move on from her childhood crush. Especially when it was pretty obvious it was going nowhere.

She sighed long and hard. Then she pulled out the elastics holding her braids in place. She ran her fingers through the soft strands, allowing them to lie flat on her shoulders. With Cam leaving for baseball camp in a week, it was time for a makeover. When her senior year started, Stella would walk the halls of Oak Hills High a brand-new person. Free to date whomever she wanted without Meatwad and Master Shake getting in the way.

ONE

INKY FINGERS

Will stared at the panel for his online comic until his vision blurred. The dorm room he lived in smelled of old sweaty socks, distracting him. No. That wasn't the whole truth. He just couldn't capture the image in his head, and it was frustrating the shit out of him. His summer hiatus was over. It was time for a new chapter. And, yet, nada. Zilch. His brain was empty.

Two hundred e-mails in his in-box impatiently asked for the next installment of *The Adventures of Morla the Witch Hunter*. And that was just in the last twenty-four hours. More came in daily. He was dropping the ball. Big-time.

Emotions moving from frustrated to pissed, Will closed his ink-stained hand over the sheet filled with half-hearted scribbles. He crumpled the subpar panel, obliterating the story line in one go. Then he rubbed his tired eyes. The fatigue from being up all night clung to his shoulders. His mind was stuck like a mammoth in tar.

He glanced up at the clock. His first class wasn't until two in the afternoon. He had four hours to bang out a page, ink it, scan, and post before he had to go. Getting a shower in there might be stretching it. At least he'd change his shirt. That would hide most of the funk. He hoped.

Sitting back in his chair and tilting his head to face the ceiling, he envisioned his MC. Morla was a badass witch hunter. She had long, black hair that trailed behind her when she ran from the Nosferatu Coven. She was tall and long-limbed, possessing an agility that helped her kill the Ifrit sent to eliminate her by the Mother Supreme. The skintight leather suit she wore emphasized the richness of her brown skin, which glistened in the sun when she had to strip down to her underwear to swim away from the vicious water sprites. Her full lips were always smirking, like she knew more than she let on, enabling her to defeat the rogue warlock terrorizing the southern village of Lapsa. But her best feature was her intensely brown eyes, as rich as the earth she walked upon. They could stare into someone's soul and determine if that person was a witch.

In the last panel he had posted before he participated in a graphic design workshop hosted by the Design Media Arts department at UCLA, Will left Morla in quite a pickle. A bind.

The most precarious situation. Basically, he was screwed. She had been poisoned by a dark witch and left for dead after she had fallen down a gully. It was the best scene he had written so far. His readers gobbled it up. The e-mails had been crazy. Readers wanted more.

Will cursed his insidious brain for abusing Morla in this way. She lay on her back at the bottom of the gully in pain. The poison slowly worked its way through her system, eating every cell in her body. How the hell was she getting out of this one?

In defeat, Will threw down his pen and pushed away from his desk. His ergonomic chair's wheels let out a *grr* of protest beneath his weight. Being a little over six feet with broad shoulders meant he carried around weight that punished furniture if he wasn't careful. He shoved his fingers through his hair. He couldn't think straight. His eyelids were so heavy. It was a Friday. He was feeling a classic case of weekenditis. He tabled updating the comic for now rather than come up with crap. What was the point, anyway? His brain was mush. His readers would just have to be patient and wait another week.

STELLA WALKED OUT of class feeling like a million bucks. She had aced her history quiz. She'd finally put in her contacts without poking an eye out. Her chin-length hair bounced like she had Beyoncé's magic fan blowing air up toward her face. And the maxi dress she had finished sewing the night before flowed like water when she moved.

All summer she had been busy with her makeover. Come the

first day of school in mid-August, she had been more than ready to unveil the new her. The Stella free from her hovering helicopter big brother and his henchman.

Shoulders squared, she approached her locker like a model walking the runway at New York Fashion Week. She punched in her combination with newly manicured nails and curled her moisturized fingers around the handle. A slide up and a tug later, the door swung open.

All Stella's confidence tumbled to the floor as fast as a trash can's worth of crumbled paper and a single banana peel spilled out from the bowels of her locker.

Laughter and the words "Trash for trash" followed the spectacle, spoken by the leader of the three girls that the school referred to as the Salads: Lemon. Romaine. And Parsley.

"This is getting old, ladies," Stella said in complete and utter exasperation. "It's getting *really* old." The last part, she muttered to herself. She didn't bother with the sigh and the eye roll that usually accompanied finding her locker stuffed with trash. Again. She didn't even feel tears prick the corners of her eyes. Patience, she reminded herself. Soon she would be a student in one of the best fashion schools, living the life she was meant for.

"Tell me," Lemon said. "Where did you get that dress?"

"Saved it from a dumpster, maybe," Romaine, her second-in-command, chimed in most helpfully.

"I see Parsley's the one in charge of locker stuffing today," said a lovely, confident, slightly sassy male voice. "Why don't you ladies go find someone else to bore with your conformity? Shoo!"

Stella smiled at her best friend over her shoulder. His hair was parted to one side and held in place by a dragonfly clip showing off the neon streak. Franklin Park wore his soul on the outside. That was what Stella loved about him. And the blue suede shoes on his feet. They were to die for.

"Would it kill you for some originality?" he continued, aiming his question at the Salads as Stella swapped out her morning books for her afternoon books. The studded-leather bag she had made just couldn't hold them all at once.

"You're one to speak, Park," Lemon said. Clipped. Like a verbal slap. "That hair is so last year."

"The Salads? Original?" Stella asked, speaking to Franklin as if the Bitches of Eastwick didn't exist. "Does not compute. I guess I should be happy that Lemon's group is as typical as it gets. Can you imagine if they were more creative with their bullying?" She shuddered.

"Don't think that just because you got rid of the braces and put in contacts that you're more than you are," Lemon said, venom dripping from her tinted lips.

Her words were quickly followed by laughs and catcalls from the horde, which reeked of expensive perfume and was clad in Rodeo Drive couture. Then, as if hearing the silent command of their queen, the hive mind continued down the hallway.

Unable to contain herself, Stella shouted after them, "You're going to beg me to make you clothes one day!"

The Salads kept sashaying like her words meant nothing to them. A part of Stella was stung, but another part became twice as determined to succeed. It was the best revenge, after all.

"Speaking of clothes." Franklin drew her attention back to him. "Are you channeling *Project Runway*'s season nine winner? That's certainly an Anya dress."

A huge, braces-less smile spread across Stella's face. "This is challenge one from the new season. The designers were asked to put their best foot forward." She twirled to show off the lighter-than-air chiffon she had used for the dress. "I went for Cali-beach girl. It's a call back to my roots. I think Tim Gunn would be proud."

Franklin clapped. "Even if we're four hours away from the beach on a good-traffic day."

Stella pouted. "I go where inspiration takes me. That's what Christian Siriano did, and he went on to become the youngest winner of *Project Runway*. I totally plan on breaking that record."

"I can't say this enough, but I really like this new confidence of yours. And from what I hear, so do half the boys in school."

"Only half?"

"The other half are head over heels for me."

She blew him a raspberry before she said, "It's definitely easier without Cam around."

"Tell me you already have a date for homecoming." Franklin's eagerness was catching as they walked arm in arm toward the cafeteria.

"I haven't decided yet," Stella confessed.

"You can't procrastinate on this. What happened to Operation Boyfriend Hunt?"

"I have several promising prospects. In fact, I already have a date lined up for tonight."

"Pray tell, just how many are these prospects of yours? I will not settle for less than five."

"As a matter of fact, there are eight of them."

"Well done!" He patted her arm. "Now, how do you propose you narrow the eight down to one?"

"That's what I need you for," she said when they grabbed trays and got in line. "You're going to help me choose."

"Oh!" Franklin perked up. "Can I make a bracket like they do in sports? I'm going to call it the Boyfriend Bracket."

"What do you know about sports?" Stella sent him a dis-believing sidelong glance.

"Enough to know there are a lot of hot athletes."

This time, Stella allowed the eye roll. The situation called for it. She didn't doubt that between her and Franklin, they'd come up with the suitable candidate for her senior-year boyfriend. And she wouldn't even have to hide him anymore. Ah, freedom. Oh, how sweet.

They picked a table in the middle of the cafeteria. The second they put their trays down, Franklin leaned forward and said, "Who are the guys? I need names."

Stella licked her lips, then looked around. "There's Tommy Larrabee, Kevin Marquez, Joey Esposito, Daniel Connors, Mike Cortez, Eric Richards, Aaron Anderson, and Hector Villegas."

"I can work with that" was all he said as he grabbed his tray and stood.

"Aren't we having lunch?" she asked, pushing away from the table, then standing.

"You eat." He waved her back down to her seat. "I have work to do. Meeting at your room after school."

"I'm visiting Nana this afternoon," she called after him.

"It won't take long" was the last thing she heard before the crowd's buzzing swallowed the rest of Franklin's words. The gleam in his eyes made tumbleweeds jump around in Stella's stomach. Suddenly she wasn't very hungry. She had a feeling what should have been a simple way of finding a boyfriend had become a tiny bit complicated.

TWO

LAUNDRY DAY

After school, Stella and Franklin sat in her room staring at the bracket of potential boyfriends. They had it propped up on an easel. Beside each candidate's name was a headshot with numbers in glitter indicating when the first date would take place. Lines extended from the names that met into one rectangle at the center, which declared the winner in sparkling letters above it. If it shined, gleamed, or sparkled, Franklin had used it. The piece of cardboard was so colorful, Stella feared it could be seen from several houses away.

"As you can see"—Franklin indicated the brackets with a ruler—"I've grouped guys that best match each individual's qualifications for a fairer assessment. There are eight in all, so that's two dates per weekend for a month then we move on to one date per week for the semifinals. And for the finals, you get to choose from the last two contenders. I predict you'll have a boyfriend by the holidays."

Stella nodded, her lower lip sticking out. "I have to say, I'm impressed. What are the stars and hearts for?"

"I'm glad you asked." Franklin beamed. "I've ranked the guys based on looks and charm. One to five stars for looks, five being smoldering. Same with hearts. One to five hearts for charm, five being charming to the max."

"What about things like attitude?"

"That falls under charm. Plus I hate anything that isn't a star or a heart. Deal with it."

Stella pursed her lips, considering. "Makes things simple. I like it."

"Good, you see it my way."

"At least now I can focus on the dresses I have to sew for the dances and making sure my college applications are on point. But don't you think this is going a little too extreme?"

He slapped the ruler on the board, hitting poor Kevin Marquez's smiling face in the process. "Extreme is my middle name. And you said it yourself. This bracket takes the pressure off."

"It certainly lowers the percentage of choosing the wrong guy. How did you get them to agree on when the dates will happen?"

"I have my ways." He arched an eyebrow at her, then he

regarded the board once more. "Since Tommy is tonight, I went from there with the other guys. Actually, you have a pretty diverse group here."

"I'm not going to like where this is going, am I?" She squinted at him.

"Hear me out." Franklin brought the ruler to each guy as he spoke. "Tommy is president of the student council. Kevin is captain of the chess club. Joey plays football. Daniel swims. Mike is point guard for the basketball team. Eric plays the clarinet. Aaron, well, he's the wild card, but he does have a band, so the artists are accounted for. And Hector is the glee club's Bruno Mars. You can actually win prom queen with this group if you wanted to."

A protracted sigh left Stella's lungs. "I don't have time to campaign for prom queen. I need to focus on my college apps, especially the one for Parsons. Plus, going toe to toe with Lemon? Who has the time? Give her prom queen. I just need to get through this bracket and find a boyfriend before all the craziness starts."

"I'm just saying. You already have the ingredients right here."

"In neon and everything that glitters from the office-supply store."

A huge smile brightened Franklin's face. "If you think this is over the top . . ." He pulled out a travel-size booklet from his messenger bag and handed it to Stella.

"What's this?" The front was as colorful as the board. She started leafing through and found the answer as he spoke.

"It's a miniature version of the bracket. Each page contains a picture of your date with all his interests and what clubs he belongs to in school. As you can see, the back of each page is blank. That is where you will put all your notes after each date so we can better assess who makes it to the next round."

"Jaw-dropping effort," she said, eyes wide.

He lifted his chin. "Thorough is my second middle name."

"I don't know anyone with a second middle name."

"Well, I do. Remember, prom photos are forever. We will find you the right guy to fit that space in the picture."

"Are you sure being a fashion designer is your goal? Because the CIA is always open to new recruits."

Franklin executed a few karate chops and said, "I can be a fashion spy. Ruling the runways by day, collecting important information for my country by night."

"All right, Agent K-Pop." She slapped the booklet against her palm. "Let's focus on finding me a boyfriend before you go and save the world from crimes against fashion."

STELLA WAS THANKFUL for three things. First, Franklin's bracketing idea was actually helpful. Now they had a clearer picture of which of the eight guys she had dates with might eventually become her boyfriend. She smirked at the idea of Cam losing his cool if he ever found out. But, to save her the drama, she and Franklin were keeping things on the down low from her brother. He was way too busy with college and baseball, so there was quite a bit of breathing room.

Second, it was a Friday, which meant no homework. Oak Hills High valued giving students rest on the weekends. For Stella, it meant more time for sewing and sketching. She needed to start conceptualizing her dress for homecoming. Not to mention the two dates she had lined up. One for that night. One for Saturday. Sundays were family days.

And third, her favorite part of Fridays were her weekly visits with Will's nana. Despite the blush that still colored her cheeks when she thought of him, she had set aside her childhood crush. Stella understood that while she had feelings for him, it was nothing more than a fantasy. Regardless of her enlightenment about William Montgomery, she loved Nana. She'd stuck to checking in, even if summer vacation was over. Not that Nana needed a babysitter—Nana's word. She was capable. Even so, Stella stopped at the store and grabbed a few necessities Nana might need.

Armed with two eco-bags worth of groceries, Stella left her modest Honda hatchback at the curb and walked up to the mint-green Victorian the Montgomerys called home. A mix of fuchsia and orange bougainvillea lined the walkway. Box flowers bloomed in a riot of color beneath the windowsill. And a swing dominated one side of the front porch.

She was so at home that, instead of ringing the doorbell, she tipped the potted azalea for the spare key. She and Nana had a great routine going where Stella entered and put the groceries away while Nana prepared afternoon tea. Then they'd gossip or talk clothes. Nana had a great sense of style, which Stella admired.

After unlocking the front door, she returned the key to its hiding place, picked up the groceries, and pushed into the house. She called out, "Nana, I'm here. I got those tangerines you like."

She pushed the door closed with her hip, then went straight to the kitchen. Its cheerful yellow tiles never failed to make her smile. More flowers and potted herbs sat above the porcelain sink on the windowsill. Setting the bags on the table, she began unpacking.

"Nana, you won't believe what happened—"

A crash startled her into dropping the canned peaches. It fell to the floor with a thick *thunk* before rolling away.

"Nana?" Stella called again. Her shoulders were up to her ears.

Usually, Will's grandmother would have responded by now. Then Stella's gaze flicked to the stove. The kettle was there, but no flames were beneath it.

Another crash made Stella jump. She grabbed the closest weapon. A rolling pin. It would have to do. A knife seemed more menacing, but really? What was she planning to do? Hack the intruder to death? She wasn't that brutal.

So, rolling pin in hand, she held it like a bat, the way Cam had taught her. At the back of her mind, a small voice told her to call 911. And run. But what if Nana was hurt? Stella wouldn't be able to forgive herself if she didn't somehow help.

She inched her way toward the laundry room, which also doubled as a storage area. It was located to the left of the kitchen, close to the back door that led into the yard. She swallowed. The door was ajar. She debated whether to call to Nana again or just charge in.

Eventually, she saw no point in delaying. Maybe it was an animal of some sort. Yeah. It could be a raccoon. Or a bear. Did they have raccoons in Oak Hills? And a bear would be worse, right? She had seen *The Revenant*.

She pushed away the grisly possibilities. Pun intended. Counting to three, Stella let out a fierce battle cry as she charged into the laundry room. A figure taller than her and less hairy than a bear yelled and slammed backward into one of the stainless steel shelves. Baking pans clattered to the floor. The crash was deafening.

In the racket, Stella raised the rolling pin.

"Slappy!" the figure yelled, arms stretched out.

Stella's pulse rocketed more than it already had, for an entirely different reason. She blinked twice, making sure she wasn't hallucinating the man standing in the cramped space. He was in nothing but his boxers. Blue boxers. Blue boxers with white stripes. Or was it white boxers with blue stripes? Her throat closed, allowing only a keening sound to escape. All the blood rushed to her head as her eyes roamed greedily over bare shoulders, abs made for superhero movies, and . . . and . . . Brain.exe ceased functioning.

Her fingers went slack, dropping the rolling pin. The tip of which landed on her big toe. The pain brought everything back online. She stifled a scream as she turned around, sure her face was strawberry red.

"Slappy?" Will asked, concerned. "You okay?"

Stella didn't know what to do. Half her brain was happy. It finally had a picture of Will in only boxers. Blue with white stripes, definitely. The other half was mortified. She was sure he had caught her ogling him. Thank goodness for her throbbing foot. The nail might have died, but it was for a good cause—regaining clarity.

"Will, what are you doing here?" she asked. "In your boxers," she added, without thinking it through. Adrenaline flooded her veins. She was practically vibrating.

"No one was home. I put all my clothes in the wash" came his response.

"Shouldn't you be at school?" She closed her eyes only to be met by the image of Will's perfection again. Her eyelids flew up. Oh, gosh. That image would definitely haunt her. For a long, long, *long* time.

"It's the weekend."

"I know that. Where's Nana?" she asked, steering the conversation toward safer avenues.

Shuffling happened behind her while Will spoke. "She had a couple of errands to run. I think she plans on making a huge dinner since I'm spending the weekend. You can turn around now."

Slowly, Stella turned and then winced. A fully dressed Will in sweats and a UCLA T-shirt rushed toward her.

"Where does it hurt?" he asked.

"My big toe," she said with a hiss. The rolling pin was heavier than it looked.

"Sit." He ushered her back into the kitchen toward the closest chair and eased her down. "Take off your shoe."

As Stella slipped the sandal off her prickling foot, Will moved to the fridge and pulled out an ice tray from the freezer. He upended the cubes onto a towel by the sink, then brought the wrapped bundle to her. He took a knee, guided Stella's foot to rest on his thigh, and placed the bunched-up towel over her big toe—already in the process of swelling. She hissed again from the shock of the cold on the pulsing heat.

"Too cold?" Will looked into her eyes.

A new wave of awareness flooded Stella's cheeks. She shook her head.

As if he saw through her bravado, he said, "Just bear with me for a few minutes. It will feel better soon." His free hand moved up to her calf and began massaging it.

Stella's lungs stopped working. Oh, it was feeling better, all right. The discomfort moved to more inappropriate places. She shouldn't even be thinking along those lines. Will was just helping her. Doing a nice thing. His concern for her well-being was pretty obvious. Nothing more.

So caught up in her thoughts was Stella that she failed to notice that Will was talking until he looked up at her again. He was so handsome. Her chest ached. She had missed him.

"Thanks for checking on Nana," he said, his gratefulness all over his expression.

"I love Nana," she replied, swallowing the sudden lump in her throat. "It's no biggie."

"Well, I owe you one. Seriously, anything you need."

Asking him to homecoming was at the tip of her tongue. It was a crazy thought. Never in a million years would Will say yes. Again Stella's fantasies were overtaking her common sense. She blamed the lapse on the toe. The pain was making her delusional.

Forcing the thought to the deepest reaches of her clearly confused mind, she said instead, "Don't worry about it."

"You cut your hair," he mumbled. He seemed to be concentrating too hard on icing her toe.

Her hand flew up to her head. "Ye-yeah. I thought a change was good." Nerves invaded her stomach. She didn't know how to feel about the possibility of Will hating her bob. It prompted her to say, "You like it longer?"

He whipped his head up so fast that Stella thought he might lose his balance. "No! Um . . . I mean . . . it's nice."

"Nice?"

And the blushes kept coming. Stella was afraid she might pass out. It had been months since she'd last seen Will. If she was being honest with her traitor of a heart, her feelings for Will were as real now as they had been then.

"What happened?"

The exclamation came from the kitchen entrance.

Will and Stella turned their heads toward Nana. She had arrived without their noticing. Ribbons were tangled in her waist-length hair. Bangles jingled on her wrist. The boho skirt she paired with a sleeveless ribbed shirt highlighted her thin frame. Pushing seventy and she looked good. Stella could only wish she would look as good when she was Nana's age.

"Rolling pin met with toe," Will said, answering her question. He lifted the makeshift ice pack and set Stella's foot back on the floor. Then he stood and dumped the ice into the sink.

Despite feeling the void Will left behind, Stella put together a bright smile. "I'm fine, Nana. I was clumsy. My toe is nice and numb." She left out the fact that her heart and mind might not be.

"It completely slipped my mind that you were dropping by today." Nana deposited her own groceries beside Stella's on the table. Will busied himself putting away what Stella had left out, then started on the contents of his grandmother's eco-bags. "You will stay for dinner. I'm making lasagna and garlic bread."

Stella's mouth watered. Nana's lasagnas were legendary. No one said no to the creamy, layered pasta. She was about to say yes when she remembered the date she was supposed to go on in a couple of hours.

"Nana, I want to, I really do," she said, already hating the idea of leaving.

"I hear a *but* coming." Nana eyed her.

"It's Friday," Will chimed in. "She probably has plans or something."

Will's words did unexpected things to Stella's heart. How did he know? And more important, would he tell Cam? Then the craziness of her thoughts caught up with her. Of course he'd think she had plans. What teen didn't on a Friday night?

STELLA SAT AT her favorite booth in her favorite diner with Tommy talking a mile a minute about how more people should be conscious of their civil rights. It was the debate team captain in him. And his passion for the Black Lives Matter movement.

She admired all those things about him. How he stood up for what was right. How he had aspirations to study law and eventually enter politics to make a difference. She should have really been paying more attention. She had ideas too. Thoughts. Opinions.

But that was kind of hard when every two sentences the image of Will's abs kept popping up in her mind. They resembled dinner rolls, he was so ripped. Shame wrapped Stella like a blanket on a chilly night. Will wasn't her date tonight. Tommy was. He was a great guy. And that smile? Who wouldn't like that smile? It was what won him the student council presidency.

What would Franklin say?

The second her best friend's disapproving expression replaced Will's abs, Stella mentally slapped herself and forced her brain to focus on the most important things: Tommy and the marginalized youth of today.

WILL PUSHED AROUND pieces of lasagna on his plate. Normally, he would be halfway through the pan of creamy, meaty goodness by now. But . . . but . . . his taste buds didn't seem to be working properly. The buttery garlic bread should have been soaking up the meat sauce and making sweet, sweet love in his mouth, but . . .

"William, where's your head at tonight?" Nana asked, finally fed up, it seemed, with his lack of an appetite.

He sighed, setting his fork aside. "When did she cut her hair?"

"You mean Stella?"

The twinkle in her eye said she knew exactly whom he meant. He nodded.

"Oh . . ." Nana rubbed her chin as if deep in thought. "About a month before school started. Right about the same time her braces came off."

That was right. When she smiled, there wasn't any metal in her teeth anymore. How could Will have missed that? He had been too distracted by the way the edge of her hair kissed her jaw. It suited her. Too damn well.

"You know she's on a date tonight," Nana said, reeling Will back from his daydream of running his fingers through her hair.

"She can do whatever she wants," he replied, biting back what he really wanted to say. He had been on dates too. None of them lasted more than the night. Hookups, really. But what could he do? The one he wanted, he didn't deserve.

"Is that so?"

He dropped his gaze to his half-empty plate. The raise of Nana's eyebrow was too honest. Too telling.

"You know, when your pappy was younger, it took him a really long time before he got up the courage to ask me out."

The mention of his grandfather was enough to lift Will's bowed head. The man had died when Will was only seven years old. He had few memories of him. So any story was welcome.

"That doesn't sound like Pappy," he said, remembering his grandfather as a confident man.

"Oh, he was a shy guy, my Andrew." A look came over Nana's face that spoke of how much she missed him. "But the important thing is, he finally got up the courage to ask me out. He needed to be honest with his feelings to get what he wanted."

Leaning forward, Will picked up his fork and started shoveling the remaining lasagna into his mouth. No matter that he didn't taste the food. It was to keep him from answering. His tongue had grown too big for his mouth, anyway.

Will knew the story was for his benefit. Being honest with his feelings? Seriously? Nana was laying it on thick. But what she didn't know was that Pappy was a far braver, far greater man. Because Will? He was taking everything to the grave. His tombstone would eventually read: *Here lies the poor shmuck who kept it to himself.*

THREE

BRACKET PARTY

The next Friday, Stella strode into her room to find Franklin waiting for her. He was hovering around the bracket board, studying the guys. They had made plans to meet and go over her date for that evening. He turned when he heard her come in.

"You're back early," he said, then frowned. "That's not good."

It definitely wasn't. It was only eight p.m. Her date had started at seven. She removed her light jacket and threw it onto her bed before she sat on the edge, crossing her legs.

"Daniel's definitely out," she said, even if she hadn't gone on her date with Joey yet. He was Saturday night. She didn't need to compare the two to make her decision of who was moving forward. "The swimming shoulders and fantastic abs are not worth it."

Franklin gave her a once-over, then looked at Daniel's photo. "What happened? I rated him four stars for looks and three hearts for charm."

"First of all, the movie sucked. I can't trust a guy with no movie-selection skills. It's going to be a long year of duds at the cinema, and you know how much I love watching movies."

"That can't be all of it. You can't disqualify someone for having bad taste."

"Says the guy who broke up with someone for wearing kigurumi onesies to bed."

He glared at her in outrage. "Don't you bring Hayden into this! He was definitely five stars, five hearts in my book. But the onesies thing? Just no! But, seriously, what happened with Daniel?"

She felt a blush coming on, but it was for the worst reason. "He kept running his hand up my thigh while we were in the cinema, so I walked out on him twenty minutes into the movie."

"What!" Franklin's eyes were so wide, Stella could see the whites. "That asshole!"

"Where are you going?" Stella grabbed his wrist as he passed her bed on the way to the door.

"I'm going to shove my shoe up his ass so far that even his future grandchildren will feel it. No one sexually harasses my Stella. No stars, no hearts for him!"

Stella smiled and squeezed his wrist. "And for that I love

you. We were bound to run into a creep in this process. Let's just hope he's the only one."

He regarded her with intense scrutiny. "Should I start chaperoning you on these dates? Because you know I can."

"And be the third wheel?" Stella's heart melted when he nodded. "You hate being the third wheel."

"I hate seeing you taken advantage of more."

She got up and hugged him. Then she said, "You don't have to do that. Just take him off the list of potentials."

"I'm also drafting an anonymous tip about him for the wall of the Shame Bathroom. Girls will want nothing to do with him after I'm done."

"Do what you must." She gestured to the board.

With chin held high, Franklin produced a red marker, drew a circle around Daniel's head, and slashed a line across it. The finality in his strokes made Stella feel infinitely better. She breathed easier as she sat back down and looked through the bracket once again as Franklin wrote Joey Esposito's name into the rectangle for the next round, right under Tommy's.

"Shame about Kevin, though," Franklin said, referring to her date after Tommy. "He had potential. That dimple. Four stars, four hearts."

"They all have potential. Why do you think we had to put them in a bracket? Although, I got the feeling that Kevin was more interested in taking selfies. Of himself. Of us. Of our food. His eyes were on his phone more than they were on my face or my cleavage."

"Makes sense. He's the official photographer of the *Oak Hills*

High Herald, or OHHH, for short." He breathed out a sigh, then looked at Kevin's picture longingly. "A shame, though. Guys seem to be running out of proper social skills in this day and age."

Stella waved at the board. "Either way, I owe Tommy another date. I wasn't entirely in the right headspace when we had dinner."

"You were thinking about Will the entire time, weren't you?" Franklin wiggled his finger at her, a suspicious gleam in his black-coffee eyes. The eyeliner he had around them gave his look a sharpness that made people pay attention.

"Not the *entire* time." She sighed. She had told him all about the laundry-room incident. "You should have seen him. Just in boxers. It was art, I tell you. Plus we have to give him credit for not telling Cam."

"How are you so sure?"

"I'm still going on dates, aren't I?"

"Don't even think of going over to the dark side again." Franklin gasped, pointing a warning finger in her direction. "We're doing this because you're moving on from this silly crush of yours. He's a no-go."

"I wouldn't call it silly. But you're right," Stella said with a lot less enthusiasm. She really shouldn't be thinking of Will. He was in her rearview. Needing a break from Boyfriend Bracket talk, she steered the conversation toward the future. "How far are you in your applications?"

"Just finishing up the essay portion. Mine's about Coco Chanel. Yours?"

"Diane von Furstenberg."

"How feminine transformative of you."

"Shut it! She revolutionized the way women dress." She tweaked his arm playfully. "I just can't believe it's finally here." She pushed off the bed and approached her desk, where all the applications were stacked. "We've been preparing for this since eighth grade. And now it's here."

Franklin came up beside her, arms crossed. "You're not actually entertaining the possibility of not getting in, are you?"

"Of course not! Because it's not going to happen. You and I are brilliant. In a year we'll be sharing a crappy apartment in one of the boroughs and studying at one of the best fashion-design schools in the country. Maybe even the world."

"You really have your heart set on Parsons, huh?"

"Why not Parsons?" A dreamy look came over her as she stared at the application. "It's in NYC, which is one of the seats of fashion. The city of Mercedes-Benz Fashion Week. Plus, their teachers are fantastic. They shot *Project Runway* there. And let's not forget the alums who have gone on to create global fashion brands. Parsons is *the* 'it' school."

"FIDM is just as good. If not better."

"You just don't want to trade California weather for blizzards and humid summers."

"My hair will not forgive me." He faced the full-length oval mirror standing in one corner of her room and checked his makeup.

Stella smiled. She and Franklin had shared the same dream since they'd met in sewing class. She was pretending to go to soccer practice while he was pretending to go to ballet class. It was New York or bust. Mecca of fashion in the country. The only reason they'd applied to other schools was because their guidance counselor made them. Something about having safety schools being a smart idea.

A *ping* pulled Stella out of her thoughts. Franklin fished out his phone from his back pocket and checked his messages. A grin formed on his lips afterward.

"I know that look," she said, barely having to glance at him.

Franklin made a sound that was akin to taking the first bite out of a decadent slice of chocolate cake. "Speaking of five stars . . ."

"Oh! Is that the guy you were telling me about? The one with the extensive vinyl collection? How may hearts was he?"

"Three hearts." His lips quirked. "I can always work with that."

She rolled her eyes. "All looks and hardly any charm. I'm surprised you aren't in a committed relationship yet."

"Commitment is for my thirties. I'm here to party. And speaking of which, my prospect just invited us to a frat one." He showed her the message.

"That's three hours away!"

"All the best parties are."

Stella wondered if she could say no. She had so much to do. Finishing her essay, for one thing. Completing her Parsons portfolio, for another. Tim Gunn would want her to stay home.

Franklin read her mind before she opened her mouth to refuse. He stood by the bracket and pointed at the fourth name on the left side. "He's going to be there."

Joey Esposito, running back for the Oak Hills Otters. Five stars, four hearts. Stella considered her options. She had a new dress to finish, but she also liked the jock enough to drive three hours. If she went to the party, she wouldn't have to go on a date with him the next day. It meant more sewing time. She moved to her closet and threw open the doors.

"Then help," she said over her shoulder. "I'm not showing up at a frat party wearing clothes from a previous date. It's bad luck."

Her sewing soulmate eagerly came to her aid. "It's a frat party, so we need something eye-catching."

"Nothing too revealing. I want to feel sexy, not like bait." She sent him a pointed glare. "Remember what Tim Gunn says about showing skin."

"We'll go with your midriff, then. Got to show off those abs while you still have them."

"Hey!"

He pulled out a light cropped sweater and a flared jean that Stella had found at a thrift store and updated. "Pair with those leather wedges."

She nodded. She might joke, but Franklin had never styled her wrong. His taste was impeccable. And his eye for fashion was always on point. If Stella ever considered anyone her competition, it was him.

"I'll accessorize with hoop earrings and multiple rings."

Franklin pursed his lips into a smile. "Perfect."

WILL TRAILED CAM into the noisy frat house. Every square foot brimmed with partying coeds. He was too preoccupied with the Morla predicament that he had yet to solve to fully appreciate the "fun"—Cam's word—surrounding him. Angry e-mails were already flooding his in-box. Fans wanted the next chapter ASAP. There were even quite a few death threats. Talk about pressure. Cam slapped him on the shoulder hard enough to wake him from his think-haze.

"What did I tell you?" he said, smug satisfaction in his tone. "Is this just what you need or what?"

"I have a paper due Monday—"

"Paper, shmaper." Cam cut his excuse off. "You've been in our dorm for a week. That's not what being in college is about, bro."

"I went to classes and—"

Cam cut him off again with, "You smell like moldy socks. You need this party. *I* need this party. Let the player out. I know he's still in there somewhere."

Will resisted the urge to smell himself. Cam didn't know what he was talking about. He had remembered to shower. He buried himself in school work and the comic because his mind kept wandering into dangerous territory.

His annoying friend gripped the back of his neck and pulled him close. "When was the last time you got laid?"

Will shoved him away. "What? You volunteer as tribute?"

"You're pretty and all, but you're not my type." Cam scanned the crowd. "Seriously, though. We need to find you a girl. Clear the pipes. You're all tense."

Will scanned the crowd once more. Maybe Cam was right. He had been tense all week. Maybe hooking up with someone was exactly what he needed. To bring him clarity. Not only to the Morla situation, but as a way to forget more complicated thoughts. Erasing images of a girl with chin-length hair and a great smile. And how hot she had become in the span of a summer.

"You know what," he said, grinning, "you're right. This party is exactly what I needed."

"That's what I want to hear! Let's go grab a drink. Then we'll scope out the selections tonight," Cam said over his shoulder as he led the way to the kitchen past the living room, where a twerking mass of people gathered.

Will followed along, already in search of some fun.

Cam pulled two cups from the stack on top of the keg and stuck the nozzle into the first one. "Foam or no foam?"

Someone else answered "Foam" as Will shrugged. He didn't care. Beer was beer. He eyed the bowls of chips on the table. No way was he reaching in. Way too many hands had done so already. He took the cup that Cam handed him and tilted his head toward the back door.

"I'll drink this outside," he said.

The pool was the best place to scope out potentials anyway. He was several yards away from the house when a touch on his arm stopped his progress. He turned to come face-to-face with a petite brunette with a sweet smile.

"You're Will, right?" she asked. "I think we have Intro to Graphic Design together."

Will considered her. "Tanya, right?"

She shook her head, never losing her smile. "Lisa."

"Lisa." He was about to smile back when all the blood in his body froze. His eyes landed on the one person he could pick out of any lineup. Will couldn't believe his eyes at first. Maybe his mind was playing tricks on him. Had he been thinking about her that much, that she'd actually materialized? But it was impossible. They were three hours away from Oak Hills. And this was a frat party. His blood boiled soon afterward.

Will was already pissed at the idea of Stella being in a place with booze and God knew what else, but now he could see she was standing by the tiki bar talking to a guy, all up close and personal. One soon to be dead meat. Their heads were so close together that Will thought their foreheads would touch. The fingers of his free hand curled into a tight fist. Then Stella did the worst possible thing: she threw her head back and laughed.

The caveman in Will didn't approve, especially when the guy put his hand on Stella's lower back. With her sweater missing that section, there were definitely no barriers between Dead Meat's palm and Stella's smooth, soft skin. He thought of Cam and how he would not approve. Yeah. The bro code. He was going to stop this nonsense for Cam's sake.

"Hey, Lisa, can you hold this for me?" He handed her his cup of beer. "I'll be right back."

He left without waiting for her reply. Nana would have killed him for being so rude, but he was on a mission. Stella had her face tilted upward with a flirty look that sent chills down his spine. The guy she was with had one hand against the bar, and the other was still on her waist. There was no doubt what was about to happen.

Lips in a tight line, Will strode toward them. Stella was unaware of him until he wrapped his hand around her arm. He tugged her away from the guy without saying a word. Stella's protest died when she recognized him. Her eyes grew wide. The guy stepped forward, but Will shut him down with a menacing glare.

"You're coming with me," Will said, after he was sure the guy wasn't going to be a hero.

"What are you doing here?" Stella asked, finally getting her words back.

"That's my question." Will leveled a heavy gaze her way. Stella had the sense to look guilty. "You're coming with me."

"No, I'm not."

But before Stella could yank her arm out of his grasp, Will hit her with the truth. "If I'm here, then you know who else is here."

She went pale. So pale that Will was afraid she was going to pass out. "But Franklin."

"Who?" Will scratched his head in confusion.

"My best friend. We drove here together." Stella licked her lips. "He's inside. I'm not leaving here without him."

The determination in her eyes did things to Will that he wanted to forget. When she licked those lips? It was impossible not to follow the tip of her tongue with his gaze. He mentally smacked himself. He was here on behalf of the bro code, nothing else.

With a clearer head, or as clear as he could get it to be without actually physically punching himself, Will ushered Stella toward the side of the house. "You stay here. What does Franklin look like?"

"Dark hair with a neon streak. Korean." Then something like aggravation came over Stella's face. "I can't believe you don't remember him. He's only been my best friend since grade school."

"Yeah, well, I bet he didn't have neon hair back then." He gritted his teeth. They were running out of time. The longer Stella stayed at the party, the more likely Cam would run into her. And Will didn't want to stay for that shit show. "Just stay here."

He left her in the shadow of the house and plunged back into the party. But about a yard from the house, he ran into Lisa again.

"Hey, where did you run off to?" she asked, still holding his cup.

Breathing in, he rubbed his lips. "Lisa, I'm sorry but I have to go. I'll see you in class?"

Her smile finally vanished as he sidestepped her.

Then remembering his task, he turned and said, "You haven't seen a guy with neon hair walking around here, have you?"

Will barely managed to dodge the beer flung at him as he ran back into the house. Well, that could have gone better. Plans of hooking up that night were officially off the table. If he knew Stella, she wouldn't stay hidden for long. He had to find Franklin before her patience ran out and she decided two people looking was better than one.

FOUR
EARLY-MORNING MILK SHAKES

Shaking from the adrenaline pumping through her system, Stella gave the keys to Franklin and asked him to drive. She sat in the passenger seat, looking out into the night in stunned silence, torn between shock at Will's sudden appearance, frustration at yet another date ruined, and relief at not having to deal with Cam. Thank God Franklin knew her well enough not to ask questions. It was a long drive. A silent one. But when they arrived at Stella's house well past two a.m., she insisted Franklin sleep over. She couldn't stand to be alone.

As they lay side by side, Franklin snoring softly, Stella stared at the ceiling. She was tired, but her brain wouldn't leave her alone. She turned her head until she caught sight of her digital clock. It was pink. It was fuzzy. And it flashed a large magenta four. In the a.m.

She pushed aside the comforter and swung her legs over the side of the bed. There was obviously no sleep in sight for her. Too much had happened. She needed to clear her thoughts before she could attempt closing her eyes again.

So down the stairs she went. At the bottom she turned toward the kitchen and padded all the way to the back door. She grabbed the small camping lamp from the counter and pushed her way outside. Not bothering with slippers, she headed straight for the old tree in the backyard. The damp grass crunching beneath her feet gave her a degree of comfort.

At the trunk, she looked up at the tree house and the NO GIRLS ALLOWED sign still dangling from the window. It used to be the one place she wasn't allowed, until her mother had forced Cam and Will to include her in their games. It had been a while since she'd visited. A small smile stretched across her face. Memories of her father building the tree house flooded her. She missed him every day, and she was glad that the tree house was a great reminder of him and his love for them.

Hooking her arm through the lamp's handle, she ascended the wooden slats nailed to the tree that acted as the ladder. She climbed through the porthole cut into the floor and carefully eased herself into the corner beside one of the windows. There were two. One on the right, one on the left. She liked the left one because it had the best view of the side of the house, all the way to the street.

With a flick of her finger, the lamp sputtered to life, giving white illumination to the space. Small shelves housed dusty G.I. Joes with Bumblebee sitting among them. A quilt still covered part of the floor, which Stella didn't bother sitting on. It needed a good wash.

So many wonderful memories were made in this tree house. They might have forgotten it over the years, but it still stayed the same. Stella could barely fit in her corner anymore. She placed her elbow on the windowsill, rested her chin on her palm, and sighed. The street and the houses around her were all quiet. Unlike what she felt. When stuff hit her from all sides, it got overwhelming. Like that night.

When she'd arrived at the frat party with Franklin, the last thing on her mind was Will. She had actually had fun with Joey. He'd listened when she spoke. He'd gotten her drinks. He'd made sure she was comfortable. Attentive and confident. A true contender in the Boyfriend Bracket. And then, out of nowhere, Will came swooping in, interrupting her date. How was she supposed to get over him if he kept popping up during unexpected times?

"Yoo-hoo," someone called from below the tree house.

Stella blinked several times. Her eyes had gone dry. How long had she been staring into the night? It wasn't light out yet, so maybe not that long? She had no idea.

She eased to the opening and peered out. Half her lips quirked up at the sight of Franklin in his silk pj's. In his hands were two giant to-go cups she recognized. They were from her favorite diner. Well, it was the only one in town. And it was open 24-7.

"Are those what I think they are?" she asked in anticipation.

"Only one way to find out," he said, grinning. "Oh, Rapunzel, Rapunzel, let down your hair, so that I may climb thy golden stair."

"Ah, handsome prince, sadly I have cut my hair. You must make do with the rickety stairs."

Franklin pursed his lips. "At least grab these so I don't break my neck on the way up?"

She reached down and eagerly received the to-go cups. As she scooted back into her corner, Franklin's head popped into the tree house. He heaved himself up and plopped beside her.

"I'm not doubting your father's craftsmanship or anything, but for the sake of my neurosis, I have to ask: Are we safe in this thing?" He pointed at the cup in Stella's right hand.

She offered it to him and said, "We're safe. This house can hold up to six kids without buckling."

"Why doesn't that make me feel better?"

"We'll be fine." She took a sip from her cup, and her eyes rolled to the back of her head. "Yum!"

"Double-chocolate milk shake," Franklin said as he took a sip from his own cup. "The cure-all for everything that ails you."

"Do you remember the time I caught the worst cold in history?" Stella asked, eyes shining.

Franklin grimaced. "A runny nose is never a good look on anyone."

"And you brought me milk shakes every afternoon after school?"

"Cured you right up."

"Thank you," she said between sips.

"Why do I have a feeling you're not thanking me for long-ago milk shakes?"

"Let's make it a blanket appreciation."

There was a pause while they focused on polishing off their milk shakes. Then Franklin finally broke the silence with, "Are you ready to talk about it?"

She swallowed and sighed. "I'm sorry that we had to leave the party early. I knew you were out with that guy you liked."

He waved away her apology. "Don't. There's nothing you have to be sorry for. Cam was there."

"Of all the parties, he would have to pick that one to attend. Just my luck!"

"We both know you're not upset over Cam being there." He looked her in the eye.

She played with the straw in her cup. "I was really having fun, you know?"

"With Joey!" His eyes grew wide. "I knew he'd be a gem."

"Yeah." She nodded, then frowned. "But Will—"

"No." Franklin stopped her before she could say anything she would regret. "Don't go down that road. He may have saved you from Cam finding out, but he did get in the way of you and Joey. He could have just said you should leave without scaring Joey away."

She nodded, seeing his logic. "Do you think Joey's a lost cause?"

"Are you saying he's officially in the next round? I mean, I know we already voted him through, but after the party he's officially in *in*?"

Pushing away all thoughts of Will, Stella gave herself fully to the process of finding herself a boyfriend. "Yeah. And add another heart to his score. He's more charming than you initially gave him credit for. Sweet too."

"Then he gets an extra smiley face too for his gallant efforts."

They laughed.

Milk shakes and best friends. What more could Stella ask for?

EARLY SUNDAY MORNING, Will drove out to the Valley View Flea Market. It was his favorite weekend hangout to score vintage comic books and merch. He was hoping to find some inspiration. A solution to his Morla problem still eluded him, and he was afraid if he didn't find one soon, his readers would hunt him down. Despite the comic being anonymous, he knew there were creative and determined people out there who might actually find him.

With the pressure mounting, he parked the truck at the open area designated for cars—a dusty field, mostly. He hopped out of the cab and stretched. The colorful sign above the entrance called to him like a siren. He had some money to burn.

He walked through the archway announcing the name of the market to all who entered. The open area space was divided by long tables and tents. All the vendors had their own piece of the property where they laid out their wares. Makeshift avenues were created. Will didn't know how the stalls were assigned, but there was an organized chaos that he liked. The buzz in the air from haggling and people browsing sang in his blood. Waking him up. He had a good feeling about this.

Relaxed, he ambled from stall to stall. His fingers went through boxes and boxes of comics, all still in their plastic. He loved the musty sweet smell that came with rummaging through aging paper. By lunchtime, his exhaustive search bore fruit in the form of a first edition *Sandman*. Signed!

He had a wide grin on his face as he strolled toward the food trucks. On his way, his eye landed on a familiar figure. Then his ears latched onto the only voice that haunted his dreams at night. He paused. How could he not? Then he turned toward the stall where she stood in jeans and a pink sweater sporting a white bow at the back, haggling with a woman holding up blue fabric with shiny beads on it.

Her name was on the tip of his tongue. He hesitated. If he walked away, she wouldn't know that he had been there. It was that easy. And, anyway, he'd gotten what he had come for. But there was still half the flea market to explore. What were the chances of running into each other if he walked away and minded his own business?

Apparently he had been standing there like a dolt for longer than it took to find an answer to his dilemma, because Stella turned around with a wrapped brown parcel in her hands, which he assumed was the cloth she had been haggling for. The wide smile of triumph on her face made his heart sing. But the moment she saw him, that smile dimmed. It was like a punch in the gut.

"H-hey, Slappy," he said, giving her a small wave. He swallowed and shifted his weight from foot to foot.

"Will," she breathed out.

In his head, he was like, "Surprise!" in the most unsure tone possible. Instead he smiled. Unfortunately, his lips wobbled. What to do? What to say? Hell, if he had an idea.

Stella broke the silence between them by asking, "What'd you get?"

He raised the comic in his hand. "First edition *Sandman*. It's signed by Neil Gaiman." Okay, he couldn't help himself. He sounded a little giddy.

"Oh." She looked uneasy. He hated that.

"What about you?" He pointed at her parcel.

She hugged it closer to her chest like a beloved teddy bear. "Fabric for my homecoming dress."

"Is it homecoming already?" Dread ran down Will's spine.

"Not for a few weeks. I still have time to put the dress together." When she shook her head, her hair moved like she was one of those women in a shampoo commercial.

Will had to create a fist to stop himself from reaching out and running his fingers through the strands. He already knew they would be soft. But she would freak. She would definitely freak.

"Okay . . . then," she said, backing away a step. "I'll just be on my way."

"No!" He caught himself. "I mean, do you really have to go?"

Was it hope that he saw in her eyes? His heart hammered in his chest. Then came the words that made him want to dance, even though he was the worst dancer in the world.

"I can stay."

He tilted his head toward the food trucks. "I was just about to grab lunch. Want to join me? My treat?"

She smiled tentatively. "I can eat."

They found an empty picnic table. Will asked Stella what she wanted and said he would go grab their orders while she saved the table for them. She didn't disappoint when she picked the pulled-pork spring rolls and the fried mac-and-cheese bites.

Why he was smiling from ear to ear as he stood in line was lost to Will. He was just ordering food. Which he was about to eat. With Stella. What was there to smile about? The sun was shining. He had scored a signed comic book. Accidentally ran into the girl he couldn't get out of his head. Small stuff. Good stuff.

All throughout lunch, Will was ashamed of having done only three things. He ate. He mumbled or grunted replies to questions aimed his way. And he stared. If Stella hadn't been so focused on enjoying her food, she would have totally caught him ogling her like an idiot.

When had Stella—Slappy with the braids and braces— become drop-dead gorgeous? He'd liked her before, but now? She was goddamn dangerous. Who knew a summer without Cam or Will would allow Stella to come out of her shell? This was bad. It was really bad.

"Oh, there's pie!" Stella said. The excitement in her voice pulled him away from his thoughts. "My treat!"

She opened her bag and grabbed her wallet. A small book fell out as she did so. Will was about to call her attention to it, but she had already scampered away to buy dessert. Curious, Will reached out for the book. It was handmade, and on the cover it said BOYFRIEND BRACKET in glittering letters.

"What the hell?" He grimaced as he flipped through the book.

Inside were pictures and information on eight guys. If Will remembered correctly, they all went to Oak Hills High. One of them had even been on the football team with him. The guy she was with at the frat party. On the back of the first four pages were notes in Stella's cursive writing.

For Tommy Larrabee, she'd written, "Give Tommy another chance. He's a nice guy. Passionate."

For Kevin Marquez, she'd written, "Cute, but too self-involved. Totally no connection."

For Daniel Connors all she'd written was "Pervert."

And for the fourth guy, Joey Esposito, she'd written, "I like him."

Those three words were the worst of them all. They were three stabs in the gut for Will. Not only was she dating, but she had a roster of guys she had placed in a bracket so she could pick a boyfriend. Most of the guys in the book were total idiots. The kind he and Cam had worked hard to scare away from her.

"Apple pie à la mode!" Stella announced like she had won a prize.

In a panic, Will pocketed the book. He winced. He should have returned it to her bag when he'd had a chance. Now he was stuck.

Instead of sitting opposite him like she had during lunch, Stella slid into the bench he was on. "Will? Don't you want the pie?"

His name from Stella's sweet voice made all the nerve endings inside him pay attention. It was like a fireworks display beneath his skin. He was too aware of her. Aware of her citrus perfume and coconut shampoo.

"Y-yeah," he said.

For the second it took her to hand him the pie, Will's gaze never left her lips. He liked how pale pink they were against her skin. He wanted to punch himself for thinking how soft that mouth would be against his. Maybe as soft and smooth as her hair? *Okay, weirdo, quit it.*

He gripped the plate so hard he was surprised the cardboard didn't rip.

"Okay." Stella settled herself beside him.

The sides of their thighs touched before Will moved to the farthest corner of the bench. Which wasn't very far. There was barely an inch separating them. Will prayed for mercy as he dug into the pie. The ice cream's coolness wasn't enough to ease the furnace that his body had become.

"Okay," Stella repeated. "You're officially acting weird. What's going on?"

It was weird, all right.

Will swallowed wrong. A coughing fit had him doubling over. Stella placed an open palm on his back and slapped him repeatedly. Sweet Jesus, it was agony. He liked her touch so much that he hated himself for liking it. He forced himself to straighten. Then he cleared his throat.

"I'm fine," he squeaked out. More throat clearing. "I'm fine."

Stella studied him with a too-honest expression. "I don't believe you."

He stifled a groan. She was stubborn like her brother. And too perceptive by half. It wasn't like he could confront her about the book. He still hadn't wrapped his mind around it. And over his dead body were they discussing how her skin was a beautiful contrast against his own and how all he wanted was to sink his fingers into her hair. But it was clear that Stella wasn't about to drop the topic, so he went with the safest reason for his weirdness.

"I'm stuck," he said, staring at the slowly melting vanilla on the half-eaten pie.

"Oh?" she encouraged.

"There's this story I'm writing." She didn't need to know about the comic. Will didn't want to discover how she would react to finding out.

"For school?"

He nodded, hating himself for lying. He was years away from storyboarding, but she didn't know that.

"I wrote myself into a corner. My main character . . ." He paused, glancing at her. He liked that he was several inches taller, despite her long legs. Okay, huge mistake since she was looking up at him with that heart-shaped face. He immediately focused on the wood grain of the picnic table. "She was poisoned and lying helpless in a ravine with no hope of rescue."

"No antidote?"

He loved how she immediately latched on to the idea. "None."

"What's your story about that your character was poisoned?"

At first, Will's heart leaped out of his chest. How to tell her? But she had no idea about the comic. It was anonymous. And she wouldn't know about his website unless he specifically told her about the link. Still, he needed to be careful.

"My character is a witch hunter."

"Wow."

Her admiration made him feel strange, scary things. "So she's faced with a lot of danger from the witches who want her dead."

"Ah, the poisoning."

"Yeah." He nodded. She was catching on fast. It was thrilling.

A cute valley formed between her eyebrows. She drew her bottom lip between her teeth. The wheels in her head were turning, and nothing seemed sexier to Will in that moment.

In the guise of waiting for her response, he watched her unabashedly. Just for this afternoon. Will allowed himself this one time to be with her. Then it was back to school and, hopefully, forgetting this version of Stella existed.

Soon enough, like the rising sun, Stella's face brightened. "What if she's immune?"

"What?" It took Will a second to restart his brain and return his focus to their conversation.

Stella smacked him playfully on the arm. "She's immune to the poison. If she's in danger all the time, it's possible that she has taken precautions against poisoning. She can still feel its effects and suffer, but once the poison cycles through her system, she'll be fine again."

Will put on his artist cap and ran through the scenario. It made sense. It was so simple. Why hadn't he thought of it before?

"You are brilliant! I could kiss you," he said.

He realized his mistake the instant the words left his mouth. The blush on her cheeks was so obvious. Stupid. Stupid. Stupid.

"Stella . . . I . . ." What was he going to say? That yes, he did indeed want to kiss her? Or apologize when a part of him meant what he'd said?

Just as he found himself about to give in to his urge to plant his lips on hers, an impish grin transformed Stella's features. She took the fork from him and skewered a bit of apple that had fallen out of the pie and brought the piece to her mouth. After she'd chewed and swallowed happily, she said, "I better get a cut of your royalties when you get famous for this idea."

Like a balloon popping, the tension broke between them. Will stole back the fork and proceeded to scarf down the last of the dessert. Saved by the pie.

FIVE

NO JOKE

By the end of the next school week, Stella was more than ready for the weekend. Franklin had been out since Wednesday for his Model UN conference in DC, and she missed him terribly. He had texted her that he had landed and was on his way back to her. And none too soon! Because she had been alone, the Salads had scented blood in the water and had been particularly vindictive that week. Wet gym clothes. Missing school books. And speaking of books, she had lost her Boyfriend Bracket booklet. Franklin was going to kill her!

She sat in the middle of Nana's living room, trying to retrace her steps. Where had she last seen the booklet? She'd definitely used it the night after leaving the frat party. She'd noticed it was gone on Tuesday. That was a lot of hours in between when she could have lost it.

"Something the matter, my dear?" Nana asked, opening a second steamer trunk filled with clothes she had collected over the years.

At the question, Stella wilted. "It's just . . ."

She was in vintage heaven, and she couldn't fully appreciate it. When she had arrived looking down in the dumps, instead of their usual tea, Nana suggested she help her sort through clothes she was planning to give to Goodwill. With the help of Will, who had decided yet again to come home from UCLA to torture Stella—that was only in her head, of course—they had moved the coffee table aside. Nana had just sent him up to the attic for the third steamer trunk. Stella might have drooled a little watching him lug those trunks.

Nana set aside the ruffled dress she was holding and inched closer, until she reached Stella's side. "It's okay. You can tell me."

"I'm just missing Franklin," she said after a sigh. "He would have loved to see your dresses. They are all beautiful. I can't imagine giving them away."

"You can have whichever you like." Nana placed her hand on Stella's. "But I get the feeling that's not all that's on your mind."

"Nana, please tell me this is the last of them?" Will asked as he entered the living room with the third steamer trunk hoisted on his shoulder, an arm around it. From the strain of Will's biceps, Stella imagined it weighed a ton.

Stella's jaw practically unhinged from its sockets as she gawked at Will. In a white T-shirt and jeans, he reminded her of those Calvin Klein ads with #mycalvins in front and a model pretty much ripping off his T-shirt to showcase not only the jeans but also his abs. There wasn't a show of abs in this case, but those biceps. It was torture. Yet she made no move to leave. She was happy right where she was.

"Just place that over there." Nana gestured to the last section of the living room floor that was free. She pushed to her feet and gave instructions. "Let's make three piles for the clothes. There is Keep, Take, Donate. Keep will be the ones you think should stay with me. Take will be what Stella wants for herself. And Donate will be the clothes for Goodwill."

"How do we know which ones are—"

"Stella will be in charge," Nana said, interrupting Will's question.

"Where are you going?" Stella asked, throat suddenly dry for no reason.

"I'm going out for garment bags. All the dresses will need them after they are sorted." Nana smiled.

Looking up at the beautiful bohemian in front of her, Stella caught the gleam in Nana's eyes, but she didn't quite understand what it was for. A part of her wanted to insist that Nana stay. Not leave her with Will. The flea market experience was enough for Franklin to lecture her for an hour straight about the merits of their bracket. The other part of her—the part where naughty thoughts came from—was glad Nana was leaving.

"You'll be fine," Nana said, as if reading Stella's mind. To Will, she said, "You mind what Stella says. She's in charge of the clothes. You're just the muscle."

Will rolled his eyes but still bent down to receive a kiss on the cheek from his grandmother. Stella's heart melted. The love was real there. It was in every molecule between them.

When the front door shut and Will returned from escorting Nana out, Stella busied herself with assessing the clothes. She wanted to keep them all, but she had no space. Plus she wasn't that selfish. She knew the feeling of finding something wonderful at a thrift store. She was willing to share.

"All right, boss," Will said, opening the third trunk. "What's the plan?"

A flood of heat rushed through Stella. She liked Will calling her "boss" way too much. She almost forgot what she'd been about to say. "Take the dresses out of the trunk one by one and see if they have any stains or rips that need repairs. Then show them to me."

"You got it, boss."

Another thrill went through Stella.

In the hopes of not spontaneously combusting, she focused on sorting the dresses. They worked in semi-silence. *Semi-* because Will would once in a while ask her opinion on a dress. The routine brought back memories of her tough past few days.

"What's wrong?" Will asked as Stella folded a white dress with electric pleats on the skirt. That one she was definitely taking.

Once again, she felt herself wilt. "Lemon Lambert's being a monumental bitch, that's all."

He scratched his cheek. "Isn't she Lance Lambert's sister?"

Her nod was half-hearted. "Usually I can take the Salads' bullying, but Franklin was out most of the week, so there's no buffer. It's stupid."

"Bullying is never stupid," he said, scowling. "You should report it."

"Seriously." She waved both her hands. "I don't want to make a big deal out of it. Mostly just trash in the locker. Hiding my books. Kids' stuff. I only need to put up with it for a few more months, then it's off to college."

"Doesn't make it right."

"Will." Her shoulders drooped.

Sensing she needed a shift in topic, Will asked, "Have you sent out your applications?"

"All but one."

"Which one?"

She bit her lower lip. "Parsons." Her stomach jiggled like jelly at the thought. She would never admit her insecurities to Franklin about getting in, but there was something about being with Will that made her feel . . . safe. That was the best word to describe it. "This school, it's just really important, you know?"

"Like UCLA was to me."

"Exactly!" She clapped and pointed. She loved how he understood her right away. "I don't want to mess up this application. One mistake and it could mean I'm not going to college for at least a year."

"You still have the other schools you applied to, right?"

"It's not the same." She shook her head. "Parsons is it for me. I need to get in."

"Then you'll get in." He said it with so much conviction that she believed him.

A smile relaxed the tight muscles on her face. She hadn't even known she was scowling until Will's reassurance talked her off the ledge. "Thanks."

"At your service."

They looked into each other's eyes. There was a pause. A spark. A moment when the air felt charged between them. If they weren't on opposite sides of the living room, Stella was sure they would have kissed. But that was crazy. Will didn't like her that way.

So she was the one who changed the topic. "Now if I can only find this book I lost, everything will be peaches."

"What book?" Will stared at her with an intensity she couldn't understand.

"It's nothing, really." She downplayed it. "Just something Franklin made for me. If I don't find it, he'll be sad." Most likely mad. But that was neither here nor there.

Still studying her, Will reached for the back pocket of his jeans and pulled something out. Stella followed his hand with her gaze. In seconds he produced something small and sparkly. She swallowed.

"Why do you have that?" she asked in a whisper. More like her voice was disappearing. Afraid of the coming consequences.

"Care to explain what this Boyfriend Bracket nonsense is

all about?" He waved the booklet like it was something to be thrown away.

"How did you get that?" Her eyes widened when she connected the dots. "The flea market. You went through my purse?"

"Of course not!" Will said in his defense. "When you grabbed your wallet to buy pie it fell out. So naturally I picked it up."

"Then why did you keep it?"

"You know Cam won't like this."

Stella felt all the blood in her body rush to her feet. "You wouldn't!"

"Try me."

There was a seriousness in Will that made her uneasy. He would tell Cam. It was part of their stupid bro code. The question was: Why had he waited this long? He'd had the booklet the entire time.

"That's an invasion of my privacy." Maybe she could guilt Will into giving the booklet back and not saying anything to her brother.

"You want this back? You have to explain it to me."

Huffing, Stella sat back on her haunches and rubbed a hand down her face. Fine. If that was what he wanted, then it was easy enough to do.

"Franklin put together a system to help me narrow down my options."

"What for?" Horror filled Will's face.

"Okay, before you judge—"

"Judging? I'm not judging."

Eyes narrowing, Stella circled a finger in front of his face. "That stupid look you have on says so."

"I just want to understand. That's all. And how this all connects to the frat party."

The sincerity in Will's buttery voice softened some of the edges in Stella's annoyance. "It's not like you and Cam never went to parties. And don't you dare say it's different, because that's totally sexist. Girls just wanna have fun."

Will pinned her with a hard stare. "But it is different."

"You're just like Cam," Stella said, disgusted. She crossed her arms and pretended not to see the flicker of hurt on Will's face.

They sat in thick silence until Stella squirmed. It became obvious that Will wasn't moving until she explained herself. So she rolled her eyes and started talking.

"Since school started, guys have been asking me out. I said yes to all of them so that I can find The One."

Will's face paled. "The One?"

"Yeah." Stella waved her hand in a dismissive gesture. "My senior boyfriend. The guy I will be hanging out with all year. He'll take me to all the dances. What were you thinking?"

"And the bracket?" he asked, as if afraid of the answer.

"Franklin put it together to help me narrow down the candidates. Homecoming is coming up. I need to lock down a date."

"What about after senior year? What happens then?"

"Why are you so interested?" His blank stare made her look up at the ceiling and say, "It's simple. I break up with him after graduation. We all know high school relationships don't last into college. Plus I'll be too busy making my mark in fashion. I just need someone to be my boyfriend for senior year. Plain and simple."

Will let out a long breath. "I can't say I understand completely, but you have to know that half the guys in this thing are idiots, right?"

She pouted. "They're actually nice when you get to know them."

He opened the book and scanned the pages, then said, "Like Daniel the pervert?"

"Well, there's always an exception to the rule."

"Give me a good reason not to find this guy and break his face?" He showed her the page with Daniel's picture in it.

"Maybe because beating someone up is not you?"

He snorted, but it was obvious from his face that she'd got him there. "I can beat someone up if I want to."

"Just give me back the booklet, please." She reached out, palm facing the ceiling.

For a long minute he just looked at her, booklet still gripped in his fingers. Stella actually thought that Will was never giving it up until he finally placed the thing in her hand. She held it to her chest like a lost doll newly found.

"I'm worried about what Cam will say if he finds out," he said.

The triumph in her chest deflated. For a second it had seemed like Will was finally on her side. Maybe even a little jealous that she was dating all these guys. But apparently she had it wrong. In the end, he was still Cam's bro. The code still stood.

It was the final nail in the coffin of Stella's hopes for the possibility of Will. All along, she had been dreaming. Franklin had been right. It was just a silly crush. Unrequited. Totally one-sided.

Feeling the corners of her eyes prick, Stella pushed to her feet. Like hell would she show Will how sad she felt. How broken her heart finally was.

"Where are you going?"

Was that concern she heard in his voice? Maybe her ears were playing tricks on her. She inhaled sharply to keep the coming tears at bay. With all her might, she forced herself to speak.

"I just remembered that it's a Friday." She waved the booklet as she grabbed her bag off the sofa. "I have a date to get ready for. Will you tell Nana I'm sorry that I had to go?"

She didn't wait for Will's response. She hurried out of there, wiping away a stray tear as she closed the front door behind her.

SIX

REGRET AND A HARD PLACE

The days leading up to homecoming were a haze of school and sewing and dates on the right side of the bracket. Stella channeled her pain and frustration into making wearable art. She was in the middle of putting the finishing touches on the skirt when Franklin ambled into her room like he lived there. In her mind, he practically did.

"Your mom let me in," he said. Then he gasped. "Oh!"

Stella sat back on her heels and studied the dress from the floor. "You think it's too much? It's definitely too much."

"Girl, you should get heartbroken more often." Franklin circled the dress form standing in the middle of the room.

"Ha. Ha. Not funny. Plus finally accepting the truth about Will does not a broken heart make."

"But you've been in love with him since—"

"Crush," she corrected. "I was in crush with him. Like you said, it was silly. Nothing more. And you will be happy to know that I have decided on Joey Esposito as my homecoming date for Friday."

"You finally picked someone!" Franklin clapped. Then he moved to the board and crossed out Tommy's name from the running.

"Might as well move forward, right? I like Joey. He's fun to be around." For their second date he had taken her on a hike around her favorite park in town. At sunset. And he had prepared a small picnic at the end. How could she not reward that with going to homecoming together?

"What about the other half of the bracket?" Franklin gestured to the other names. "Have you decided who goes to the semifinal?"

"Move Mike Cortez and Hector Villegas up." She went back to work hand sewing the final details without looking at the board. "They are both solid four star, four heart guys."

"You got it," he said, adding the names to the next set of rectangles. "And this way Aaron can write a song about you, and he'll become famous like Taylor Swift."

Stella's lips curled into a half smile. Franklin sat on the floor beside her and threaded a needle. She pointed at a section of the skirt, and he got to work. She loved that she never had to ask. She always did the same when she was over at his place.

After they worked in companionable silence for five minutes, Franklin said, "Sent in everything. You?"

"All but one. Just making sure my portfolio for Parsons is perfect. I'll send it next week."

"Perfection is in the imperfections. I think they'd rather you send in your most honest work."

"That's what I'm doing." She bit the corner of her lower lip. "I'm just making sure it's as perfect as I can make it."

"You better get a move on if you want to hear back by January."

"I'm nervous," she confessed. No matter how confident in her talent she felt, Parsons was *the* school. "What if—"

"No!" Franklin snapped, waving a finger at her. "You're not starting that in front of this gorgeous dress. You and I are getting in. Believe it!"

His conviction banished all her uncertainties. There was no plan B. It was fashion school or working at the mall until she could reapply or join *Project Runway*. Preferably, she wanted school first, then reality TV. But whatever path would get her to where she wanted to be was worth considering.

"You like the dress?" she asked after snipping the thread she'd used. Only about a couple inches remained dangling from the needle.

Franklin took the scissors from her and cut his thread too. "You'll be best dressed, that's for sure. The Salads will kill themselves."

"Even Lemon?"

"Especially Lemon, the sour witch." He pushed to his feet

and dusted off his skinny jeans. "I can't believe you scored such beautiful fabric. I really need to hang out at flea markets more. If only I wasn't allergic to cheap junk and desperation."

"Hey, don't knock flea markets. They're the best." She pushed down the memory of Will brought on by the mention of that day. She stood and stretched, working the kinks out of her neck. "I'm just happy I finished it on time. I honestly thought I bit off more than I could chew with this one."

"A corset bodice and a full skirt will do that. How many layers of tulle do you have under there?"

"Fifty dollars' worth."

"It looks like it. Oh! I almost forgot the reason I'm here."

"And I thought it was to lend me moral support. You know, like any good friend would?"

"Better." Franklin winked. He produced a folded piece of paper from his bright electric-blue jeans, which matched his hair.

She unfolded the paper to discover it was a flyer. "What's this?"

"Duh! Read it."

"A fashion show?"

Franklin snatched the flyer from her hands and rattled off the details. "It's open to all amateur fashion designers. You enter one piece. The audience gets to vote. And the winner gets a full ride to FIDM." His eyes were so wide, Stella thought they would fall out of their sockets. "A full ride!"

"You're not seriously thinking of participating," Stella said. She'd never had to worry about paying for college. Her parents had been good enough to create a college plan for her when she was born. She thanked her mother. Apparently, the practice was common in the Philippines. "What happened to 'we're getting in'?"

"That hasn't changed." Franklin waved the flyer. "I showed you this because I thought it would be fun. Even if we don't need the scholarship, participating is still experience. The more we put our work out there, the better. It's in March. And the deadline for entries is still far from now. You have time to think about it."

"I already thought about it. And it's a no for me."

She didn't feel the need to prove herself. And the show was at UCLA. That was Will's turf.

"Do what you want." Franklin's pout told her more than his words.

Stella sighed. "Fine. I'll consider it."

No. Not really.

FOR THE REST of the week, all Will wanted to do was kick himself. If only it were anatomically possible. He had messed up. Royally. For a moment, he had thought Stella trusted him when she explained the Boyfriend Bracket. Then he had to go and mention Cam. Immediately he saw the hurt in her eyes, the walls going up. Whatever chances he'd had—not that he was seriously considering a chance with her—were officially obliterated. All because he was being his dumb self.

Cam stormed into the dorm room they shared, slamming the door. It was so hard, Will was afraid it would fall off its hinges.

"What's got your panties twisted?" Will asked.

Nostrils flaring, Cam paced the tiny space. His fists opened and closed. "Just heard. That little jerk Joey Esposito is taking Stella to homecoming. Joey Esposito!"

A bitter taste coated Will's tongue as he forced himself to say, "I heard he's a nice guy."

What the hell was he doing defending the guy for? Of course she'd chosen him. She wrote in that stupid booklet that she liked him. Getting a guy was never Stella's problem. And any guy who didn't find her attractive was wrong in the head.

"He's on the football team," Cam said, scowling deep.

Will turned away from the panel he had been drawing and faced the fuming guy heating up their room. "What does that have to do with it?"

"I don't trust football players. Actually, any athlete of any kind. All they have is sex on the brain."

Will really wished he hadn't said that. A knot formed at the pit of his stomach. "I was on the football team."

"You're different," Cam growled.

"Thanks?" Will didn't know if he should have been flattered or insulted.

"Did you know she cut her hair?"

Feigning ignorance, he asked, "Who?"

"Stella!"

"People get haircuts all the time, Cam," he pointed out, sounding as chill as possible. Nothing good came from further agitating an enraged bull. Cam might have been shorter than

Will, but he was brawny. "You just got a trim last week. If Stella wants to cut her hair, then she can cut her hair."

"This is not the time to joke, bro." Cam continued pacing. Will could actually hear him breathing. "I can't chaperone her on Friday. Got practice for the exhibition game coach set up."

Like a miracle from heaven, an idea popped into Will's head. A very stupid idea. The worst idea in the world. But he was already talking before his brain could stop him.

"I'm free this weekend."

Cam paused, his eyes narrowed at Will. "What are you saying?"

Will swallowed, reminding himself to act cool. Bulls went for the soft parts when provoked.

"Look, Stella's been having a tough time at school. She's being bullied by these girls. And she's worried about getting into college."

Cam's breathing calmed some, and his pacing paused. "How do you know all of this?"

"She told me when I went home to check on Nana. We were helping her donate dresses. Anyway, that's not the point. All Stella wants is to have fun."

The bull calmed, rubbing his chin. Will saw the gears churning in Cam's head. "She'll still go no matter what I say," he said.

Will nodded, solemn. "She's a senior now. You know it's an important year with lots of dances."

Cam's jaw twitched. "More dates."

"Exactly." Will rubbed his sweat-damp hands over his knees.

"But if Stella were to go with someone you trust. Someone who wouldn't make any moves on her. Just act like a bodyguard/male-deterrent . . ." He let the sentence trail off.

The silence in their room was so complete that Will could actually hear someone snoring in the next room. But he waited. The idea had to come from Cam for his plan to work. Meanwhile, Will's heart was attempting to burrow out of his chest.

Finally, the light bulb Will was waiting for turned on in Cam.

"You have to be her date," Cam said. "You're the only one I can trust. And everyone still respects you over there. If you're with Stella, no one will dare bully her anymore, or ask her out." Then concern spread over his face. "Is that cool? I know I'm asking a lot."

"It's cool." Will kept his expression blank even as he imagined a tiny version of himself dancing inside his head.

Cam clapped him on the shoulder. "You're really doing me a solid, bro. I'll go call Stella right now and set things up." Will was about to breathe a sigh of relief when Cam turned around and said with a smile, "It's not like Stella is one of your random hookups, right?" Then he turned and left.

The second Cam was out the door, Will let the hurt that his friend's words brought go through him. What had he done? In Cam's eyes, he was just a player. Also not good enough for his sister. But he was already in it. Might as well see the plan through.

Homecoming was in a day. He needed a suit, a tie that matched her dress, and a corsage. So much to do. He grabbed his wallet and keys and hurried on his way.

SEVEN

WELCOME HOMECOMING

Will adjusted his tie again while he sat on the Pattersons' couch. He waited for Stella to come down. He may have arrived too early, both excited and nervous. He had no idea how Stella took Cam's matchmaking scheme. She had agreed, so maybe she wasn't as pissed as Will had thought. Then again, he had no idea what to think.

Hopefully the tie was the right shade. She had told him during their lunch at the flea market that the fabric she had scored was for her dress. He remembered colors well. As long as she hadn't changed her mind. On the coffee table sat a clear plastic box that contained a pink orchid corsage. The delicate flower reminded him of Stella's lips, soft and full.

Will hooked a finger into his collar and tugged. On the drive over, he had toyed with the idea of actually telling Stella everything. Coming clean. How he was going to do it, he had no idea whatsoever.

"Here she is!" Mrs. Patterson declared as she descended the stairs.

Jumping to his feet, Will adjusted his jacket so it sat properly on his shoulders. He smoothed down his tie and ran the palm of his hand over his hair. With a quick exhale to settle his heart, he grabbed the corsage and moved to the bottom of the stairs.

His breath caught at the sight. Midway down stood the most gorgeous girl he had ever laid eyes on. A silver pin kept her hair behind one ear. Her makeup was simple yet captivating. And the dress. She had transformed the fabric she had bought at the flea market into something magical.

It hugged her waist. The puffy skirt stopped above her knees, showing off her long legs. He couldn't take his eyes away from the sexy strappy shoes.

A throat was cleared. By whom, he had no idea.

As if waking up from a dream, Will lifted his gaze to meet hers. What was breathing? What was standing? Will felt lightheaded. The floor felt less solid beneath his feet.

"Well, don't just stand there." Mrs. Patterson waved for Stella to come down the rest of the way. "We need pictures."

Stella rolled her eyes as if the entire process was annoying. But Will saw the excitement on her face too. She loved this stuff.

When she reached the bottom of the stairs, Will eased the orchid out of its box. Smiling, Stella lifted her left arm. He slid the band over her hand and secured it on her wrist while Mrs. Patterson documented the momentous event.

"It's beautiful," Stella said, with a softness to her voice that drew Will in.

"You're beautiful," he whispered into her ear. Seconds later, goose bumps covered her arms. He bit down on a smile.

Mrs. Patterson took the plastic box from him. Will placed a hand on the small of Stella's back. They both smiled for the pictures. Then Stella reminded her mother there were more dances and more pictures to be taken.

They both said their good-byes. Mrs. Patterson reminded Will to drive safely, that they should both have fun, and to have Stella home by eleven.

Will guided Stella to his truck, waiting at the curb. She didn't pull away. It gave him hope. Maybe, just maybe, he had redeemed himself in her eyes. He opened the door for her and helped her up. Only when he drove away from the curb did he feel that everything was going to be all right.

SITTING ON THE passenger seat of Will's truck, Stella's knees knocked together. Her hands shook while she sent a text to Franklin that she was on her way. She had never been this nervous before. It was all too much. When Cam had called letting her know Will was taking her to the dance, she had been speechless for the longest time.

"How've you been?"

Will's sudden question startled Stella. She dropped her phone. It clattered to the floor. But before she could scramble for it, Will's phone rang. She yelped. Her heart beat wildly. It made her chest feel small.

To get her attention, Will squeezed her hand. She immediately looked to him. Cam's name flashed on the small screen. Will tapped the green circle.

"Hey, Cam—" Will began, but her brother was already interrupting him.

"Did you pick her up already?"

Stella's already too-small chest tightened further at hearing her brother's voice come from the truck's speakers. "I'm here."

"Hey, little sis!" he greeted her. "Sorry I couldn't be there tonight. You have fun with Will, okay?"

"I'll make sure she does," Will said, a wide smile on his lips.

"Not too much fun, I hope?"

A muscle jumped along Will's jaw. "We'll be fine. Don't worry about it."

"Cam, don't you have something better to do than check up on me?" Stella asked, annoyance creeping up on her previous nervousness.

"Oh, right!" her brother said as if remembering. "Got to go. Will, take care of her, okay?"

He hung up before anyone could reply. Stella had kept her eye on Will the entire time. She noticed his shoulders stiffen. What was that all about?

Will's clearing his throat pulled her out of her thoughts. "Don't pay him any attention. Cam's just being Cam."

"Can we please not mention him tonight? I mean, I already said yes to this, didn't I?"

"What do you mean?" He gave her a sidelong glance.

Stella lifted her hand. "Come on. Let's not pretend that this isn't some scheme by Cam so that I don't have a date for homecoming. You're technically a babysitter."

"That's not true."

"Oh, really? Because it looks like a massive cock block to me."

The truck swerved. Will steered it back straight. Thank goodness there weren't that many cars on the road with them.

"Will!" Stella grabbed the sides of her seat. "Are you drunk or something?"

"Can you please not say that?" he asked. More like barked, actually.

"What? Cock block?"

Again the truck swerved. Stella cursed.

"Will, get a grip!" she shouted, breathless. "Okay, okay. I won't say *it* again. But after tonight, I'll be lucky if Joey ever speaks to me again."

Will eased his foot off the gas and maneuvered the truck onto the side of the road. He cut the engine and flicked on the hazard lights. He thumped the back of his head on the seat and closed his eyes. For a long minute, no one spoke. No one moved. Stella watched Will, confused. She had no idea what he was thinking.

"Okay," Will finally said. He sat up straight and turned in his seat to face her. "Do you really like him?"

Stella's eyebrows shot up. "Joey?"

Will blinked at her a couple times. "Who else? Because if you do, then I'll go talk to him and fix this so he's your date tonight."

"You'd do that for me?"

"Yes."

Eyes narrowing, Stella circled a finger in front of his face. "But what about Cam? You know he's not going to like that I went with Joey instead."

He rubbed a hand down his face as if in an attempt to erase what Stella saw there. "I'll make something up. Cam will just have to deal."

"You'll break the bro code for me?"

Will let out a long breath. He stared out into the night. Taillights passed them, streaking red in the dark. The inside of the cab was cozy. Their only illumination came from the flashing hazard lights and the bright beams of cars driving by. It felt nice—the silence and being in Will's truck.

A part of her still worried that Will would rat her out to her brother. Yet another part of her wanted to trust Will. He was willing to be her date to homecoming. That had to count for something. The fluttering in her stomach hoped so.

If she closed her eyes, she could pretend Will was driving her home from their date. That he would walk her to her door. They would say their good-nights. Will would walk away. But before she could go into the house, he would run back, grab her by the waist, and kiss her. And the kiss would be hot. The hottest kiss in the world.

"But . . . ," Will said. "If you can go to homecoming with me instead, that would be really cool."

Still caught up in her daydream, Stella thought it was the Will in her imagination speaking. But her eyes were open. She was in Will's truck. She twisted around.

"What?" she blurted out with a laugh. "If this is some kind of joke, it's not funny."

Will faced her again. "No joke."

"I don't believe you."

"I'm serious. This is legit."

Stella stared at him, dumbfounded. This was a sick prank. She was sure of it. Like the time Will and Cam had convinced her that the small green chilies her mom brought home from the Filipino grocery specialty store were candied. When she bit into one, her mouth had burned so bad. Only a mouthful of condensed milk had stopped the pain. She'd cried all afternoon.

"Did my brother put you up to this?" She glared at him. "Is this some kind of test?"

"Not a test."

"Then why?"

"Because I can't stand seeing you with another guy." The words fell out of Will's mouth like he was serious. Like he actually meant what he was saying.

Stella shook her head, making a mental note to have her hearing checked. "I think I'm having a stroke. What does it mean to have a stroke? Can teenagers even have a stroke?"

"Slappy." Will grabbed her hand and squeezed it. The warmth of his touch snapped her to attention. "I've liked you since junior year. I never did anything about it. I knew you were safe from guys because of Cam."

"Why now?" She couldn't believe she was actually playing along. Will liked her? For years? Crazy. They must have died during the moment Will swerved the truck, and this was some sort of parallel universe where everything, even the impossible, was possible.

"Why not?" There he was, asking the right questions. "You know me. I'd never hurt you."

A shiver went through her. In the dark, everything seemed intimate. Yet she couldn't let go of his hand. This was everything she had always wanted. Will. Her date. Those two had never seemed mutually exclusive before. If she hadn't been sitting down already, she was sure her legs would have given out from under her.

STELLA WAS WALKING on air as Will led her into the Oak Hills High gym. Banners congratulating the champions hung from the rafters. The entire space was decked out in the Otter colors of blue and white. Balloon columns and arches filled the space. Tables with blue tablecloths and white folding chairs were arranged around the dance floor. To the side stood the DJ, playing music from his booth.

Already the night was magical. She could feel all eyes on her and Will. Of course! William Montgomery was a catch. All her dreams were falling into place. The fantasy turned real and Cam-approved. She didn't care how, just that it did.

"Well, well, well, well, *well*," said Franklin as he approached them in his velvet tux and violet bowtie. He had his date in tow, in a suit with no jacket and violet suspenders. "Do I even want to know?"

Stella answered Franklin's eyebrow raise with one of her own. "I'll tell you about it later." Then she faced her date. "Will, as you already know, this magnificent creature is Franklin."

"Her best friend, and I will go Korean Bruce Lee on you if you hurt her." He shook Will's hand.

Will barely hid the wince from Franklin's grip as he said, "I plan on making sure she's happy from here onward."

"Good." Then Franklin introduced his date, who offered to get them all drinks.

They commandeered a table in the middle and took their seats as the gym continued to fill with new arrivals. Classmates and their respective dates.

"Is Lemon here?" Stella asked Franklin, her eyes roving the gym.

Franklin leaned closer. "I saw her go to the bathroom with Parsley."

"Good, she's here."

She and Franklin shared a look while their dates sat oblivious to their machinations. Stella didn't feel petty for wanting to shove her amazing date down Lemon's queen-bitch throat. She considered it payback for all the trash stuffed into her locker, wet gym clothes, and nasty comments.

"I know that face," Will said, poking Stella's cheek when she turned toward him. "That face scares me."

A giggle burst out of her despite her efforts to appear unaffected by the contact. "What face? I'm not making a face."

"It's her scheming face," Franklin chimed in.

"Traitor," she said out of the side of her mouth.

"Give it up, Slappy. What are you up to?"

Franklin arched an eyebrow at her, and she sent him a look that conveyed she'd tell him the genesis of the nickname later. It was enough to mollify him into explaining what she had planned.

"Please say you know who Lemon Lambert is?" he asked Will.

"She's the one bullying Stella." He grew serious. "Why? What's happening?"

"Lemon's had the biggest crush on you, and being Stella's date tonight . . ."

Will filled in what Franklin had left unsaid. "Is a way to get Lemon back for the torture."

Stella dropped her gaze when she felt her face heat up. "I don't mean to use you like that. Okay, maybe I do. It's just that the best form of revenge is success. I never thought you coming tonight was possible, so I told myself I would become super famous instead. But that could take years. And you're here now, with me. So . . ."

Will put on a stricken expression. "That's so low. Making me feel cheap."

Mortified, Stella said, "I'm sorry! Forget about it. Lemon doesn't matter. I didn't mean to ruin the night."

Will's mask of indignation cracked, and he burst out laughing. "You should see your face right now."

She shifted in her seat. She should have never brought up her revenge plot. She was being dumb. And childish. Then Will took a deep breath and pushed away from the table. Panic sparked in Stella's chest.

"Where are you going?" she asked.

Will stood and reached down for her. "If you want better visibility, then I suggest we dance."

"What?" Stella stared at his palm and blinked. "You're not mad."

"Why would I be? If Lemon is as bad as you say she is, then she deserves an eyeful of you and me looking like we're really into each other." He inclined his head toward the dance floor just as a slow song filled the air as if on cue.

"What are you waiting for?" Franklin nudged her shoulder.

Sheepish, Stella took Will's hand and pushed her chair back. She rearranged her skirt as they walked toward the dance floor, Will leading the way. From the corner of her eye, she spotted a familiar blonde in a dress too extravagant for homecoming.

"Lemon, three o'clock," Stella said while she smiled. She could feel the leader of the Salads' glare from across the gym.

Without moving his head, Will slid a glance toward the direction Stella indicated. "Then let's make this count."

He twirled Stella before bringing her close. She gasped as her body pressed against his and they began moving to the music. Their gazes locked and everything else melted away. It became just Stella and Will in that gym, on that dance floor.

"I have to be honest about something," Will said after Stella successfully followed his lead. "I did some research on dates."

She scrunched her nose. "Why'd you have to do that? This is homecoming. There's nothing to it."

"Please don't remind me." He grimaced.

"This should be easy for us. We already know each other."

"That's why I did some research. Dates are all about getting to know each other."

"But we already know way too much about each other," Stella said, finally catching on. "Oh. Yeah. That kind of defeats the purpose, huh?"

"I thought to change things up a bit."

"Okay. I'm curious." She lifted her chin to look up at him. "What do you have in mind?"

"Instead of telling each other three things about ourselves, why don't we share three things we know about each other."

That gave Stella pause. Oh, gosh. Will may have confessed, but she hadn't yet. Her feet began to sweat. She already knew what she wanted to share about him, but a bout of shyness prevented her from speaking.

"I'll start," he said, taking the burden away from her, which Stella was grateful for. "When you set your mind to something, you won't stop until you get it done."

She felt her cheeks grow hot. "No."

"Remember the time we teased you about the monkey bars?"

The "we" Will meant included her brother, who lived to tease her. He justified it as his brotherly duty.

"I practiced every afternoon until I made it all the way to the end without falling."

"You were so proud. We were too. We just weren't showing you."

"Ugh!" She smacked his arm. "You two are such jerks. Seriously."

"The second thing . . . ," Will continued. "You secretly love broccoli but only pretended to hate it because Cam couldn't stand the stuff."

"And is my brother aware of that fact?" She shifted her weight to the balls of her feet. "Not a thank-you to this day. Ingrate. Mom stopped serving broccoli because of me. I'm surprised you know that about me."

He tapped the tip of her nose. It lifted a giggle out of her.

"Only because every time you ate at Nana's, you cleaned your plate of the broccoli," he said. "And asked for seconds."

A deep blush spread across her face from cheek to cheek. She ducked her head, using his shoulder to hide. She had no idea he'd noticed.

"What's the third thing?" she forced herself to ask despite the whirlwind in her chest. She was happy. And confused. And totally fighting to stay solid. Did he like her more than she liked him? That was impossible. She got dibs on liking William Montgomery. She had lost count of the times they'd secretly got pretend married when she played wedding with her dolls.

He lifted her chin as they continued to dance. Stella searched his handsome face for answers.

"The third thing is . . . ," he said, not breaking eye contact. "You are the most real person I know. You show all your emotions. You aren't afraid to express yourself. No matter how much we teased you growing up, you never lost that smile of yours—braces and all."

Stella felt a sting start at the corners of her eyes. She was seriously going to break down. At the gym. While dancing. During homecoming.

"Can you be any more perfect?" she managed to say around the tightening of her throat.

He shrugged one shoulder. "Depends on who you ask. Nana always gets this pinched look when I forget to pick up after myself."

Will spoke with such adorable contriteness that Stella burst out laughing. Her voice drew the attention of her classmates dancing alongside them. But she couldn't stop. Will watched her, silently smiling until her composure returned.

"Now it's your turn," he said as patient as Buddha.

There was so much hopeful expectation in his voice that Stella turned into a bundle of nerves. Oh, gosh. This was it. But before she could stumble on her feet, Stella admonished herself for being a coward. This was her chance. Will had put himself out there. Why couldn't she? If there was a time to show Will her feelings, it was now.

Reminding herself who she was with, Stella gathered her courage and said, "You're the nicest guy I know."

"That's not always the most flattering thing."

"Ah, but the entire school agrees with me. You're even nice when you break up with someone."

"Come again?"

"Clara Hutchinson. Sophomore year. You two dated for six months. You broke up with her, and she didn't even write your name along with *die* on the wall of the girls' Shame Bathroom."

"Shame Bathroom?"

She clapped her forehead. "Don't tell anyone. It's a secret."

"Now I'm more curious."

"It's the west wing bathroom. The one at the end of the hallway. The walls are filled with names of guys who other girls should stay away from and why."

"Okay, I'd rather not know what's on those walls. Thanks." He rubbed his jaw. "I didn't think you knew about Clara."

Stella raised an eyebrow as if to say "Really?"

Will let out a bashful chuckle. "I guess we weren't exactly hiding it."

"Um . . . you two were making out in the parking lot. Every day."

"I'm sorry?"

"No, you're not."

"I'm not. Clara was a good kisser."

"Why did you break up?"

He just looked at her for the longest time until she finally got the answer. Surprised, she pointed at herself. He shrugged.

"The beginnings of it. This." He gestured at the both of them.

She blushed for the hundredth time. Being with Will. Surreal. This was actually happening. She had to keep speaking or she would never finish.

"Anyway, I only brought up Clara to emphasize the fact that you're kind. Tolerating my brother is already a good enough reason to call you a saint."

"All right, all right." He raised a hand. "I get it. What's the second thing?"

"You're popular because everyone likes you," she said, while making sure to keep up with his steps. "Not because you're a jock. Not because you're mean. You actually make everyone feel like they have your full attention when they are speaking to you. All the girls love you. All the guys want to be you. Not even the bullies touch you."

"I thought that was because of Cam," he said, self-deprecating.

"And the third thing," she said, not breaking eye contact with those intense gray eyes. "You are loyal and reliable. Anytime Nana needs you, you're there. Cam calls you at midnight to sneak out, you show up."

"You know about those?"

She twisted her lips. "There's very little I don't know about you, William Montgomery."

"Oh?"

Taking the challenge in his tone, she squared her shoulders. "Real talk?"

He nodded, studying her like she was the most beautiful piece of art. Stella let go of feeling self-conscious and went with the truth.

"I've had a crush on you since I understood what having a crush meant. I even asked my mom to explain the meaning of the word to me."

Will's eyes widened. "What?"

"Sure, you and Cam always made fun of my braids, and the braces and the glasses, but in my mind, you were always the guy. My first crush."

"Are you serious?" He paused, catching himself. "I mean, do you mean it? You like me too?"

Before Stella could even finish nodding, she was swept up into Will's arms. He twirled them around and around until she was laughing. Just like in the movies. When he put her down, she was breathless and flushed. He was too.

Franklin and his date danced over to them, and he said, "Lemon just stormed out of the gym."

"Mission accomplished," Will said with a silly grin.

In Stella's mind, those words had a whole different meaning.

WILL HELD STELLA'S hand the entire drive home. To remain on Cam's and her mom's good side, they'd decided sticking to curfew was for the best even if Will never wanted the night to end. Stella had confessed to liking him back and for far longer. He was both happy and humbled by the revelation. His heart grew two sizes too big. The night couldn't get any better.

When they arrived at her house, he helped her out of his truck by placing his hands on her waist and lifting her to the ground. The smile she gave him was heart-stopping. He took her hand and brought it up to his lips, kissing her knuckles. After he succeeded in lifting a blush on her cheeks, he walked her to the front door.

She turned to face him and said, "Tonight was a total dream come true."

As if reading his mind, she'd taken the words right out of his mouth. "I honestly don't want it to end. Seeing you in that dress. Dancing and laughing with you. Hanging out with your friends. All of it was pretty amazing."

Even in the dim porch light, her blush was enchanting. He cupped her cheek and ran his thumb over her cheekbone where the color was most prominent. She leaned into the touch, looking up at him with those doe eyes. There was total trust there that he vowed never to break.

His gaze wandered to her lips. They parted as if to say something. Everything in Will begged him to bend down the few inches that separated them and kiss her. It was all he could think about since the second he'd seen her coming down the stairs that night. And from the way she looked at him, it was pretty obvious she wouldn't say no to a kiss good night. But her mom was a door away. And they had been incredibly lucky to have been given this chance by Cam to be together, whether he knew it or not. Will didn't want to push it.

So, against what his heart wanted, Will listened to his better judgment and dropped his hand. Then he took a step back. Concern replaced the desire on Stella's beautiful face.

"I should go." Will hiked a thumb over his shoulder.

Stella blinked in confusion. "Oh . . . okay."

"I'll text you," he said as he began walking back to his truck.

"Oh, okay," she repeated, but with a different intonation. Annoyance, maybe?

Will got into his truck and started the engine with the intention of driving away. He should have kissed her. He should have pressed her up against the door. He should have kissed her like he wasn't scared at all. What was he doing?

Making up his mind, he turned off the engine, got out of the truck, and ran through the yard.

Stella must have been watching him through the window because before he reached her front door, she was already out on the porch. She opened her arms and he ran straight into them. He lifted her up just as their lips met. She wrapped her arms around his shoulders, standing on her tiptoes.

The kiss was everything he'd expected and a whole lot more. It was like electricity was exchanged between them. She was soft. And sweet. She smelled of vanilla and honey. The feel of her against him brought every nerve in his body to life. She became the flame to his spark. Her touch connected them on a level Will had never experienced with anyone before. Then she parted her lips. Will was right on the edge and ready to fall. Magic was real, and it was being kissed by Stella Patterson.

"Now that's the way to say good night," Will said, trying to catch his breath.

"I wouldn't have forgiven you if you drove away," Stella replied, breathless and slightly dazed.

Will continued holding her in his arms while her fingers tangled in his hair. He'd never known a single kiss could change a man. He pressed his forehead against hers.

"I think you just broke me for all other girls," he whispered, their exhaled breaths mingling.

"That good, huh?" she teased.

"I can't feel my legs anymore."

They laughed. It was a fantastic sound to Will's ears. Nothing could be more perfect than that moment. Their first kiss.

EIGHT
NO TREATS, JUST TRICKS

Stella hummed as she ran the hem of the skirt of her costume through her sewing machine. Franklin was on the floor, sewing beads on a vest. Halloween was right around the corner, and she was in charge of their costumes that year. They alternated from year to year, and it was her turn. She didn't mind. She loved making costumes. This year she was going as a fallen angel, and Franklin was going as the Mad Hatter. The Johnny Depp version, of course.

It had been a week since homecoming, and every time her phone buzzed, her heart skipped a beat. No matter what she was doing, she would stop, pick up her phone, and check her messages. Most of the time they were from Will. They had been texting nonstop since that amazing kiss at her front door. Sometimes it was a simple exchange of hellos. Other times Will would send her a funny meme, and she would send one back in response.

This time, when her phone buzzed, Franklin beat her to it. He grabbed it out of her hand.

"Hey!" She reached for the phone and he danced away, punching in her access code. In that moment she hated having given him those four digits.

"I knew it!" he said, as if discovering a new way to sew a pleat. "No wonder you've been putting off the next dates on the bracket. You've been texting with Will!"

Stella jumped to her feet from her sewing machine and grabbed the phone back. "So what? They're just friendly texts."

"Like that 'friendly' kiss?" He placed his hands on his hips.

She paused, blushing at the memory. "There was nothing friendly about that kiss."

"So are you two official now?"

"We haven't talked about it."

All the bluster in Franklin's expression deflated. "Look, I'm not trying to meddle here, but I'm scared that you're going back to your old pining ways with him."

"It's different this time." But as she spoke, her words sounded hollow to her ears. "Something changed between us at homecoming. I think this really is it."

Franklin must have seen the doubt creep into her expression, because he gathered her into a tight hug. "Just continue to keep your options open, that's all. Go on those dates. Mike and Hector are waiting for you to set something up."

Stella let out a long breath and soaked in the comfort Franklin was giving her. "All right. I'll text Mike. Maybe we can have coffee after we finish here."

"That's all I'm asking."

AFTER TWO WEEKS and a couple awkward coffee dates with Mike and Hector—on separate occasions, of course—Stella found herself sitting on Nana's porch swing with Will. She was more confused than ever. Franklin kept encouraging her to continue with the bracket, but every time she read a text from Will, all her attention shifted to him.

"That's the thing I miss," Will was saying.

"What?" Stella blinked as if waking up from a dream. "What do you miss?"

"Nana's cooking," he said with a laugh. "You weren't listening, were you?"

She sat up straighter, which pressed her shoulder against Will's arm. An electric zing went through her body, like every time they'd touched that night. She was so aware of him. Like every cell in her body was at attention when he was within a yard of her.

"Sorry." She twisted so she faced him. "I guess I was just distracted by something. Tell me again. I promise I'm focused."

Their eyes locked. He reached up and cupped her cheek with his palm, running the pad of his thumb over her cheekbone. It was a simple touch, but Stella felt it all over. Then he leaned in. Like magnets calling to each other, she felt the pull of him. But the second her lips touched his, an aching sense of wrongness made Stella turn away so his lips grazed her cheek instead.

"What's wrong?" he asked, pulling back.

She sighed in frustration. "I don't know what's going on between us."

"What do you mean?"

"This." She gestured at the both of them. "I felt something change between us at homecoming."

He held her hand in both of his. "I did too."

"Then what are we? Because right now we're text buddies who kiss on occasion."

"Slappy, don't be that way."

Unable to stand his touch in that moment, she pulled away. "Just so you know, I'm still going on my bracket dates."

"What?" His posture went rigid. "Why? I thought that was all over."

"Because I don't know. Are we dating?" There, she'd said it. He knew she wasn't the type to mince words and beat around the bush. Franklin was right. Stella didn't want to catch herself in a pining spiral over Will again. He needed to let her off the hook if they weren't happening.

Will leaned forward, resting his elbows on his knees. He rubbed his clasped hands together. Stella waited. She needed to. No matter how long it took. She promised herself she wasn't walking away until whatever was between them was settled.

Finally, reluctantly, he said, "Do you know why I helped Cam scare away your boyfriends?"

She held her breath. This wasn't exactly where she thought their conversation was headed. "The bro code."

He shook his head. "It was because I was afraid that you'd fall in love with one of those idiots and I would never get my chance."

"But you never did anything about it, though. Up until homecoming I never knew that you had feelings for me."

"That's because I never thought I was good enough to date you."

Something inside Stella's chest pinched. She raised her hand to lay it flat on Will's back but hesitated at the last second. She clutched her hands together on her lap instead. How was she supposed to respond? She understood where he was coming from. Cam made it pretty damn clear that no guy was good enough for her. Unfortunately, it seemed like Will believed her brother's brand of bullshit.

STELLA FACED HERSELF in the mirror, pulling on the lace gloves that matched her fallen angel costume. The wings lay on her bed with the mask. Those she would put on last. It was Halloween night, and she had a date with Hector. He was the winner of the semifinals of his side of the bracket. They were supposed to meet at the house of a classmate, who was throwing the biggest party of the year.

"Do I have enough glitter on my face?" she asked when

Franklin stomped into her room. "Well, don't you look handsome, Mr. Mad Hatter."

Frowning, he threw his cane onto the bed. "My date canceled. I refuse to go to the party dateless."

"Oh, thank God." She picked up her phone. "I'll let Hector know I'm canceling too."

"You don't have to do that," he said, but it was clear from his tone that he didn't mean his words. "It's your favorite holiday, and you're nearing the finals of the bracket."

She pressed Send. "Right now, what matters is we're together tonight. How about some pints of ice cream and a horror movie marathon?"

"Ones where the hot guy dies a gruesome death?"

"Slasher movies it is!"

Franklin smiled at her. "You're a good friend."

TO SAY WILL was confused was an understatement. A week ago, when he and Stella had parted ways, it hadn't exactly been on good terms. He'd told her he didn't think he was good enough to date her. She hadn't said anything. Yet when he'd sent her a text the next day, she'd responded. She had even sent him a picture of herself in her Halloween costume with a caption saying she was staying in. She was a sexy fallen angel, and Will hated that he couldn't get away to visit her. He had a major paper due.

"Are you even listening to me?" Cam asked from his bed.

Will winced. He had completely forgotten that he wasn't alone. "Sorry. I spaced out."

Cam tossed a baseball in the air over his head and caught it with his glove. "The Halloween party at Kappa Kappa Gamma. Where's your head at?"

Will went with the truth. "Just checking on Stella."

"How's my sister? I'm worried she's going out tonight, being Halloween and all. She loves today."

"She's not going anywhere."

"How do you know?"

"She texted me that Franklin's date canceled. Apparently they're making a night of it and staying in."

"How are you two suddenly texting buddies?"

A lump formed in Will's throat. How to respond?

"I gave her my number before I dropped her off at home on homecoming. I check on her just to see if she's doing okay. You know, with the bullying and all," Will said when he was sure his voice wouldn't crack. The image of Stella in her costume turned him on so much, he was surprised he still had blood in his brain.

"Hey, thanks, bro. You're going above and beyond. I'm glad someone else is looking out for her, you know?" Cam caught the ball one more time before he sat up. "We're going to that party."

"I think I'm going to pass." Will stretched. "I'm beat and I still have that paper to write."

"Don't make me use the bro code."

"Come on, man."

"You come on. You think my sister is the only one who has had it tough? I'm beat and I want to blow off some steam. We're going to that party."

It was fast becoming clear to Will that Cam was a dog with a bone.

"It's just, it's not like you to turn down a party and some action. I miss the old days. You're my wingman," Cam continued.

Will's chest tightened, preventing him from breathing properly. "Look, I wasn't lying about the paper. But if going to that party really means so much to you, then we'll go."

Cam stood up and slapped him on the arm, grinning. "That's the Will I know." He ambled to the door. "I'll grab us some costumes."

STELLA PUT ON her lace mask and asked, "Are my wings crooked?"

"Shouldn't they be?" Franklin asked back. "You are a fallen angel, after all."

She thought about it for a second. "You're right."

"I usually am." He tipped his top hat and twirled his cane.

"You're loving your Mad Hatter costume way too much," Stella pointed out as she tugged up lace gloves that matched her mask.

"An original Stella Patterson. Of course I'm loving it. Next year I'm in charge of the costumes." Franklin balanced the cane behind his shoulders.

"I'm sorry that our plans changed," she said solemnly. "I know you wanted to hang out, just the two of us."

"Hey, I never turn down a party." He winked.

"Good." She pressed the lock button on her car's key fob, and the lights blinked twice. "Come on. The sorority house is that way." She pointed down the block and moved in that direction.

"Tell me again why we're here?" Franklin followed her with a bounce in his step.

"We're saving Will from my idiot brother's clutches. You should see his text." Stella handed over her phone. Will's message was already on the screen.

"*Cam wants me to go to this lame party. Sad emoji,*" Franklin read aloud. "If that isn't an obvious cry for help."

"You mock, but Will is helpless against my brother."

"Just so you know, I'm not totally sold on surprising Will in this way. You're blowing off a date with Hector for this."

"I blew off Hector for you. And this is as much for me as it is for Will. I didn't like how we left things last week." Stella twirled a blue strand of her long wig. "Cam won't recognize me in this, and I get to spend time with Will. Two birds, one Halloween party."

Franklin danced a circle around her as they approached the house with a sign up front that announced to the world the Greek letters for Kappa Kappa Gamma. "As your best friend, it's my responsibility to be the practical one when it becomes clear your head is too clouded by dreams and expectations. Unless you and Will make it official, then nothing is real in the eyes of the discerning masses."

"Downer."

"Thank you." He wrapped an arm around hers. "Now let's save this soon-to-be boyfriend of yours from this lame party."

Stella smiled. It seemed Franklin was finally coming around to the fact that maybe, just maybe, there was really something between her and Will. Something inevitable. Like a gardener pulling out weeds to allow the flowers to grow, Stella was willing to put in the work. Now if she could only get Will on the same page. . . .

The party was far from lame. Stella had to hand it to the sisters of Kappa Kappa Gamma. They'd turned their house into a murder mansion, complete with a corpse on the porch, a torture chamber for a living room, and bloodcurdling screams mixed in with the dance music.

A guy in a Zorro costume holding a red cup ambled over to them and declared, "You're definitely sent from heaven to find me."

She grimaced at the awful pickup line, but Franklin beat her to the refusal.

"Hell no," he said, resting the top of his cane on Zorro's chest.

Zorro smiled and eyed Franklin with great interest. "Wanna make out?"

At first, Franklin was shocked. Then he eyed the guy, who had potential, Stella could see. Just lame at picking people up.

"Let's grab a drink," he said to Zorro. "I want to find out how many hearts and stars you are before any lip-locking can commence."

"Drinks are this way," Zorro said, gesturing toward the back of the house and heading in that direction.

"You going to be okay?" Franklin asked her. "Because I'm ready and willing to stay."

Stella clamped his shoulder. "Go. Have fun. I already ruined part of your Halloween by dragging you here. I'll go find Will. Text you when I'm ready to go."

"Take your time" were Franklin's parting words as he disappeared with Zorro into the bowels of the house.

Stella shook her head, grinning. She envied Franklin's lack of inhibitions. He went where he wanted, when he wanted. And no one told him what to believe. He was his own person through and through. But it wasn't like she was a prude. In fact, she had plans. Just as soon as she found Will.

She wondered if he was in costume as she passed a sexy nurse pretending to whip a guy dressed as a tiger on all fours on the coffee table. Knowing Cam, Stella was sure he'd required costumes. Her brother loved Halloween as much as she did.

The kitchen was a bust. Only scary red punch with gummy fingers, along with other fake dismembered body parts. Stella liked the torso chip bowl, though. Extra creepy.

Moving on to the makeshift dance floor in the common room, Stella finally found what she was looking for. Or should she say who?

Will was dressed as a pirate. Complete with stuffed parrot on his shoulder. He stood by the mantel, talking to someone dressed as a drag queen. Stella just wasn't sure if he was a he or a she or the other way around.

A smile stretched across Stella's face as she ambled toward them. Will didn't notice her at first. But the drag queen gave her a once-over. Definitely a guy. The protruding Adam's apple said so. Only then did Will glance at her.

"Care to dance?" she asked in a super-sexy voice.

It took him a long second to recognize her. She had sent him a pic of her costume, so she knew he knew what she was dressed as. But considering the dim lighting, she forgave his brain's slowness to catch up.

"Ste—"

"Shh!" She placed the tip of her finger on his lips. "Tonight, I'm a fallen angel."

A grin spread across Will's handsome face. Even in an eye patch, he made Stella's knees grow weak. He took her hand in his and kissed her palm.

"Have you come to save me?" he asked, a naughty twinkle in his eye.

"Depends. Do you think you're worthy enough?"

His eye widened. He removed his eye patch. Something like desire sparked in those brilliant grays.

"Will you come with me?" he asked. "There's something I want to show you."

She nodded, entwining their fingers together. Her heart was in her throat. He led the way out of the house.

"You go, bro!"

They both froze at the sound of Cam's voice above the music and the buzz of the crowd. Stella stayed absolutely still, head tilted down so her wig fell like a protective shield, as Will turned to face her brother and gave him a thumbs-up. Cam let out a howl.

"Let's get out of here before your brother recognizes you," Will said from the side of his mouth.

A thrill went through Stella. "I don't think he will."

"I'm not taking chances. Come on, the art building is this way."

"The art building?"

"Yeah, there's a computer lab on the first floor." He walked at a steady pace, and Stella had to match her steps with his just to keep up.

"Using a computer isn't exactly the romantic idea I had in my head," she said, slight disappointment in her tone.

"Oh, you'll change your mind after you see this." He looked over his shoulder at her. "At least I hope."

Down for anything as long as it was with Will, Stella urged him forward. They passed several drunk Halloweeners on the way, and each time Will shielded her from them. Her heart sang. He didn't have to protect her, but she loved that he did.

The art building was about a block away from Kappa Kappa Gamma. She and Will climbed the front steps. He opened the door for her and bowed for her to enter. She executed a curtsy before stepping inside.

"It's the first door to the right," he said.

Stella stopped at the door he mentioned. He opened it and pointed at the first computer. He pulled out the chair and motioned for her to sit. Then he bent over the screen and typed in his username and password.

"What do you want me to see?" she asked as he typed in the address of a website on the search bar and clicked Enter.

In seconds she was led to a home page for an online comic. "What's *The Adventures of Morla the Witch Hunter?*"

"It's something I've been working on for years" was Will's reply, his eyes on the screen.

"What does this have to do with tonight?"

"Just read it. If you still want to date me afterward, then I'm willing to go there with you."

Eyeing him skeptically, Stella tapped the Enter button in the middle of the webpage.

WILL HAD NO idea how he managed to sit still the entire time Stella read. It was his open letter to her. She was never supposed to see it. Hell, he wasn't ever supposed to confess. But hey, it was a year of firsts.

While he waited, he bit the side of his tongue. He wanted to ask her what she thought. He kept sending her sidelong glances, checking her expressions. There were moments she scrolled through. Then she paused. He had no idea why. The suspense was killing him. Like any artist, he wanted her to like it. Did she? Or did she hate it?

He didn't like thinking the second thought. Because if that was the case, he might as well throw in the towel and forget his dreams of becoming a graphic novelist. Then he'd become a doctor, like his parents.

"Slappy," he said. He was unsure if he should have broken the silence. But he couldn't wait anymore.

The "Shhh" she sent his way killed the rest of his words. The air between them was still. They were the only ones in the computer lab. He rubbed his damp palms against his jeans. He breathed in deep, then let the air out slowly. He tried hard not to make any other sound.

It was several painful minutes later when Stella finally lifted her head. She stared at some point in front of her. Again, Will was left wondering what he should do. He hadn't thought things through when he'd brought her here. But he had meant every damn word he'd said about dating her. He wouldn't have shown her his homage otherwise. The ball was in her court. He was terrified of what she might do with it. All he knew for sure was he wouldn't have been able to live with himself if he hadn't at least tried.

Restless and nervous, Will said, "Lay it on me. I can take it." He hoped he could. For all he knew, he'd be a crying mess afterward.

"Morla is me," she finally said, awe and confusion clear in her tone. "But she's badass and cool. I'm not like that." She faced him, gesturing at the screen. "Is this how you see me?"

The crease on his brow eased. "Morla goes after what she wants. You're like that. You've been preparing for fashion school since ninth grade."

"Eighth, actually," she corrected.

He smiled. "Eighth. Morla knows her goals. She completes her missions with stubbornness. You won't let anyone get in the way of designing clothes. If that's not badass, then I don't know what is."

"She's really me?"

The earnest way she asked was enough to break him in half. He took her hand again.

"We don't always see who we are," he began. "It's only when those closest to us reflect who we are do we understand the truth. If you ask me? I think I didn't do you justice in Morla. But I'm definitely trying in every panel I draw."

Her gaze dropped to their clasped hands. Then she shifted her eyes to the screen again. "You started this when I was a sophomore."

"Yeah."

"That's when my boobs finally came in. Makes sense."

Will grimaced. "Don't be creepy."

"I'm being creepy?" She pointed at herself.

Groaning, he ran his free hand down his face. "You're right. I'm a predator. You should stay the hell away from me."

Stella giggled. "I think this comic is the sweetest thing anyone's ever done for me. It's beautiful work, Will. And the poisoning. That afternoon at the flea market. It was for Morla."

His heart soared. She liked it. She really did. A weight lifted off his shoulders; he was so glad he didn't have to keep the comic a secret anymore. In an absentminded aside, he said, "Cam doesn't know about this."

She grew serious. "Then maybe we shouldn't do this."

"Don't say that. We have to try."

"It's too risky."

"When did risk ever stop you? You're the girl who jumped off a cliff before any of us."

"Don't remind me. It was higher than I thought."

"This is you and me."

She grinned. "You're seriously willing to risk your friendship with my brother just to date me?"

"When you put it that way . . ."

She smacked his arm. "I'm serious."

He sobered. "Stella, I can't stand seeing you with someone else. I've liked you long enough to know that if I don't throw my hat into the ring, I'll regret it."

When she smiled again while shaking her head, he knew he was making progress. But he kept his guard up just in case she had more excuses. He knew them all. He had played out every scenario. Many of them ended with his horrible death at the hands of Cam. Even with that in mind, he wasn't willing to play it safe anymore. Stella was worth it. Her smile. Her laugh. Her touch. All worth it.

He would give anything for thirty minutes, thirty days, thirty years with her.

"When did you become such a romantic?" she asked, half kidding, half serious.

"Meet me at Nana's tomorrow and you'll find out. I have plans."

"Oh, you do, huh?"

He nodded.

She sighed, losing all her humor as the breath left her lungs. His brow furrowed. He waited for the inevitable.

When she pierced him with those soulful brown eyes of hers, he was sure she would break his heart one day. If she agreed to date him, he was all in.

"Real talk?" she said.

"Okay."

"This . . ." She pointed at herself and then him. "This is exclusive. I'm not open to sharing. I'm not playing around."

"My kind of relationship."

"All right," she breathed out. "Then it's settled."

"I guess it goes without saying that Cam can't know," he said.

"I'm cool with that," she answered. "What time do you want me at Nana's tomorrow?"

NINE
THANKSGIVING MISGIVING

"That movie was awe-some!" Stella declared while sitting in her favorite booth in her favorite diner, sipping her favorite milk shake, on a date with one of her favorite people. Bright eyes. Even brighter smile.

Will shook his head and smiled. "I have to be honest, I never pegged you as a Marvel movie kind of girl."

"Uh! That is totally sexist! I'm a DC girl too. I don't discriminate." She pointed at him. "Girls can watch all the movies we want and be just as big of fans as you can be. You're forgetting that when *Wonder Woman* came out, there were female-only screenings and all the guys were butt hurt about it. So please!"

"I'm loving this side of you. Why did it take me this long to ask you out?"

At first, Stella didn't know how to react. A part of her wanted to blush profusely. But another part of her knew the reason why they had been officially going out only recently. All the weekends after Halloween, Will made it a point to come home, not only to visit Nana, but also to take Stella out on dates. They had been having the time of their lives, discovering new things about each other with each date they had gone on. Like this day. Will had just discovered Stella was as much of a comic-book geek as he was.

The awkwardness stretched between them until Stella decided to change the topic. "What are your plans for Thanksgiving? Tell me you're coming back here."

Will was in the process of drinking from his strawberry milk shake. He swallowed, then grimaced. "I've been wanting to talk to you about that."

"What?" Her heart sank. "Don't tell me you can't come."

"It's not that." He waved both his hands. "Cam and I can only stay for the night. Our schedules are packed, and we have to drive back to UCLA the next morning."

"Setting aside the fact that I completely forgot my brother is coming home . . ." She rolled her eyes and Will chuckled. "That's all we have?"

Will reached out and took her hand in his. "Hey, however many hours it is, we'll make it count, okay?"

"So no Black Friday bodyguard, huh?"

"I completely forgot about that!"

It was tradition. The day after Thanksgiving, it was Will and Cam's mission to protect Stella, her mom, and Nana while shopping on Black Friday. They also ended up carrying all the bags.

"We have to skip this year, sorry," Will said, but it didn't seem like he was sorry at all. More like relieved, really. But Stella let him off the hook as he added, "I'm really looking forward to your mom's adobo. I wait for it all year."

"It's not like she can't cook it at any time," Stella teased.

"Yeah, but it somehow tastes better on Thanksgiving."

She laughed. Adobo was a traditional Filipino dish, the basic ingredients of which were soy sauce and vinegar. The meat could be pork or chicken or a combination of both. Stella's mom told her that what made the dish special was—no matter how simple—each family had a different way of preparing it. A recipe that was unique to the family. She loved that.

Stella grew serious for a moment. "Did you know that my dad used to say he fell in love with my mom because of her adobo? That after one bite, he knew he was going to marry her?"

Will's expression softened. "It's been seven years now, hasn't it?"

She nodded. "Yeah, but he'd been sick for a long time before that. I think in the end we just wanted his suffering to be over, you know?"

"Yeah." And Will did know. His parents worked with people suffering on a daily basis. Which was why Stella was comfortable sharing such a vulnerable moment with him. He had been there all throughout. He was as much of a witness to her father's eventual decline as her family was.

"I think that's why Cam is so protective of me," she added. "He took Dad passing away really hard." She reached out and held both his hands. "But in the end, I'd like to think that Cam just wants me to be happy. That's why you shouldn't worry. I want this." She squeezed his hands. "You and me. Okay?"

"Okay."

But when he spoke, his smile did wobble. Stella accepted that. They had a long way to go. Eventually Will would understand that it didn't matter what Cam thought. What mattered was they were together.

WILL FOCUSED ON his phone to keep from jumping out of his skin. He sat in the passenger seat of Cam's Honda Civic on the way back to Oak Hills. They had decided carpooling was best since they had to get back to campus the day after Thanksgiving. Deadlines were tight.

"I can feel you from all the way over here," Cam said above the Metallica. "Why are you so nervous?"

"Just excited," Will mumbled.

Actually, he was both. He and Stella had spoken about keeping things low-key between them when he arrived at her house that day, but he wasn't sure she 100 percent agreed with him. There was a gleam in her eye that made him suspicious. Oh, she smiled and nodded, but even with verbal confirmation, he would still have been cautious. They had to play this safe. Their families always celebrated Thanksgiving together. Nana was already there, helping with the turkey.

So, to keep from overthinking things, he focused on his phone and waited like a kid participating in the marshmallow test. He figured, like the test, if he delayed his gratification then he would be rewarded. Thanksgiving dinner was their first hurdle as a secret couple. The December holidays were coming up, and they needed to look as if nothing were going on between them or else it would all be over.

An hour out of town, Will checked the e-mails sent from his comic's server. They were mostly fan mail. In order to maintain his anonymity, he didn't reply to any of them, but one in particular caught his attention. He clicked on it and scanned the text.

"Holy shit!" he blurted out when he reached the end.

"What?" Cam looked his way.

Cam didn't know about the comic. From Will's inner circle, only Stella knew. And eventually Franklin because she insisted on never keeping secrets from her best friend. This, of course, made Will feel guilty because now he was keeping two huge secrets from Cam.

"Um . . ." Will took a deep breath. He went with the most probable reason Cam would buy for his outburst. "My professor liked my paper and e-mailed me to say he wants me to call him so we can chat."

That was close enough to the truth. Substitute professor for agent and paper for comic.

"Cool" was all Cam said, before returning his full attention to driving.

Will had to reread the e-mail several times. Almost immediately, the first person he wanted to tell was Stella. She would freak. A part of him thought it might be some prank. But he recognized the agency. Once upon a time, Will toyed with the idea of sending the comic out for either representation or publication. But he had been anonymous, and having it published sort of defeated the purpose of the secrecy. Now an agent had actually approached him. He would still have to verify the validity of the e-mail, of course. But to have *Morla* published?

Breathing became difficult. Will couldn't believe what he was reading. The number below the agent's name begged him to make the call. But he couldn't do it in the car. Not where Cam could hear. Not anywhere anyone could hear. Especially when he was going to spaz like a dweeb. He nibbled at the side of his thumb. What if Cam found out? No, he couldn't think about that. Anyway, what was the harm of one call? It wasn't like he had to commit to anything afterward. He was happy with the current state of *The Adventures of Morla the Witch Hunter.*

STELLA GLANCED AT the clock. Any minute, Will and her brother would walk through the front door. She had estimated their arrival based on Will's text letting her know they were on the way. Barring traffic, they'd be on time.

With every minute that passed, her nerves grew tenfold. She had never been this excited to see Will. During previous Thanksgiving dinners, all she'd felt were the normal jitters that came with seeing her crush. Having dinner with him. All that. But this time was different. She was dating her crush. And it was a secret. Only two people outside of Will and Stella knew. Franklin, because of course he should know. And Nana. She'd caught them making out on the couch one afternoon when they thought she had been out on an errand. All she'd done was smile knowingly at Will and say, "Carry on." Then she'd left them alone. They must have laughed for a good thirty minutes out of sheer relief.

To keep from obsessing, she focused on setting the table. Will had made her promise that they would keep things casual. But how exactly was she supposed to do that when all she wanted was to show him off? In some circles of Oak Hills High, dating William Montgomery was considered an achievement of the highest order. How was a girl supposed to keep that to herself? It was like winning the gold medal at the Olympics and not being able to tell anyone about it. But she had said she would try. And try she would.

Once the table was set, Stella headed into the kitchen. Her mother and Nana were hard at work. Had been since the crack of dawn. The turkey was in the oven. Potatoes were mashed. Corn buttered. Green beans steamed. And the adobo was simmering in the pot. The smell brought a wide smile to her lips. Her first Thanksgiving with Will. Sort of. As in dating. She pushed down as much of the giddy joy as possible.

She was about to ask what she could do to help when the front door opened and shut.

"Camron's home!" their mother exclaimed as she was checking on the turkey.

Nana made a similar exclamation about Will. Stella's heart jumped. She hurried from the kitchen to catch her mom hugging Cam and Nana hugging Will, then they switched. Both guys were all smiles. But Stella's eyes were all on Will. It might as well have been an eternity instead of a week since she last saw him. Her heart leaped when he smiled. She had missed him. More than she thought someone should ever miss another person.

Without thinking, Stella walked over to where Cam and Will stood.

"Hi!" she exclaimed, her voice higher than it should have been. She threw her arms wide and hugged Will, giving him a kiss on the cheek in the process.

She realized what she had done the second she pulled back— Will's face was beet red, and Cam, her mom, and Nana were watching them. So, turning toward her brother, she repeated the same action. A squeal of a "Hi" and a tight hug ending in a kiss on the cheek.

"You're happy to see us?" Cam said, eyebrow raised. "Normally you'd be stomping on my foot by now."

"I just missed you guys," she said, hopefully covering up coming on too strong.

Thank God her mother saved the day by saying, "Dinner is almost ready."

"Can we help with anything?" Cam asked, shrugging out of his light jacket.

"No!" their mother said with a curt wave of her finger. "Do you remember the last time you were in my kitchen?"

Cam's shoulders came up to his ears. "I was making you breakfast."

"And almost burning down the house. So, no! You go watch your game."

Unfazed by their mother's abrupt tone, Cam gave her a salute and made his way to the couch. The TV was already on before Mom and Nana reached the kitchen.

"I'll go grab us some snacks," Will said. He walked past Stella, not making eye contact.

With shaking knees, Stella followed along. The look on Will's face said it all.

DINNER WAS AWKWARD. For Will, anyway. The rest of the table seemed fine. Somehow he'd ended up sitting beside Stella, and he hadn't been expecting that. Normally he sat between Cam and Nana.

He couldn't even enjoy his adobo. His stomach was in knots. He pushed pieces of pork around. His tongue felt like sandpaper, unable to taste anything. Stella kept touching her leg against his. And every time that happened, he'd jump and pull away.

Eventually, he leaned toward her and whispered, "Cam is like three feet away. Will you stop doing that?"

She didn't respond. Instead her shoulders stiffened. There was no thigh touching after that. She didn't even look his way anymore. Instant guilt assaulted Will. She looked so pretty in that pink sweater too. The skirt showed off her legs. Had she dressed for him? He wanted badly to find out.

"Everything okay?" Nana whispered as she leaned closer.

"I'm fine," he said back.

"You've barely touched your food since we started."

"I'm not that hungry." He pushed away from the table, not sure why, but he had to be somewhere else. Everyone paused and looked up at him. Quickly, he picked up his half-empty glass of soda. "Just need ice."

Nana pushed away from the table and grabbed her own glass. "Me too."

Stella's eyebrows came together. Will turned and shuffled to the kitchen, Nana hot on his heels. Sounds of dinner resumed.

"I find it hard to believe that you're not hungry," she said when they reached the privacy of the kitchen.

"It's not a big deal," Will insisted, filling his glass with ice he didn't particularly want.

"Sometimes people don't say what they actually mean."

"Nana, don't."

"You will have to tell everyone eventually." His grandmother ignored the warning in his tone and studied him like her gaze knew the truth. "She deserves to openly show her affections for you. As do you."

"Well, we all know that's not going to happen. Can we drop it?" When she scowled at him, he added, "Please?"

"I did not raise a coward."

Will sucked in a breath. He locked eyes with Nana. There was a hint of annoyance in her eyes. She was right. He knew she was right. But the timing was wrong. It was obvious Stella was hurt. He had to do something about that.

A seed of determination grew in Will. He wasn't leaving this house knowing Stella was upset with him. Glass cooling in his hand from the ice, he made his way back to the table. Glancing at Stella, who was still resolutely ignoring him, Will settled in to enjoy his adobo. After all, he was going to need the energy to come up with a way to make Stella happy again.

"Eat up," Nana whispered into his ear as she sat down, reading his mind like she always did. "Warriors always need their strength."

For the first time that night, food began tasting good again. He even got seconds.

STELLA EXPECTED THE guys to eat their desserts in front of the game. Nana and her mom were busy putting away leftovers. She had been content to wash the dishes by herself. Unfortunately, she had an unwanted assistant.

"You don't need to be here," she said, pulling on rubber gloves.

"I'm happy to help" was Will's resolute reply.

The cheer in his voice set her teeth on edge. She plunged her plastic-gloved hand into the sink filled with soapy water and grabbed a plate. With the brush in her other hand, she scrubbed vigorous circles on its surface, ridding it of leftover gravy and cranberry sauce and a layer of porcelain. Then she handed the plate rather aggressively to Will, who took it—almost dropping it—and placed it in the dishwasher. She was committed to ignoring him.

On the third plate, Will said, "I'm sor—"

"There's no need. I was wrong. You were right" was Stella's caustic reply.

"Is that it, then?" Will asked casually. Like he didn't have a care in the world.

"Of course. You said we needed to be careful. I was obviously way too excited to spend this Thanksgiving with you. So yeah, all my fault."

"I wasn't—" Will took a deep breath, looked over his shoulder, then modulated his voice before continuing. "What I'm trying to say here is I was wrong."

"Oh, so suddenly you want to flaunt that we're dating?" Stella rubbed a plate so hard that suds were flying everywhere.

Will shoved the plate she handed over harder than the others into the dishwasher. "Look, when you kissed me on the cheek earlier, I was taken aback. I wasn't prepared for it. Good save, by the way."

"That's not what it looked like from where I was standing. You were about to hurl."

"I was in shock. Why do I even need to defend myself?"

"I get it. Cam was there." Stella turned her head to face him and whisper-hissed, "So what are you even doing here? Shouldn't you be in the living room pretending I mean nothing to you?"

"Stella, don't be this way. I'm trying to make amends here."

She looked away from the sincerity on Will's face. "It's just . . . I'm sorry, too, okay? It's hard keeping this just between us."

"I know. I know." Even with damp hands, Will still combed his fingers through his hair. Unruly strands fell over his forehead. "Don't you think I want to shout from the rooftops that we're dating?"

"What about my brother?"

"If you stop interrupting me, I'll tell you."

Stella focused on the crystal glasses next. She tried to be gentle. To break one was to invite the wrath of her mother. They were a set and used only on special occasions.

Will took her silence and ran with it. "Cam can't know. You and I agreed. But I didn't mean to be distant today. In fact, I actually have great news I wanted to share with you."

"Oh?" Stella hated how hopeful she sounded. She should be ice-cold. Ice-cold! Not falling for his words.

"I got an e-mail from an agent today. He wants to represent the comic."

"What?!" she burst out, almost dropping a glass.

"Shh!"

They both looked over their shoulders. Thankfully, no one was in the kitchen with them.

Stella modulated her voice. "You mean, like, an actual agent?"

"Yeah," Will said. "He said I should call him."

"You should! You definitely should," Stella encouraged, practically bouncing on her feet. "I'm so happy for you!"

"Yeah?" He gave her a shy smile.

In her happiness, Stella checked if the coast was clear one more time. Then she jumped to her toes, placed a quick kiss on Will's lips. He sucked in a breath in surprise. But instead of pulling away like he had done, he smiled. A bright smile. The kind of smile that showed all his feelings all at once.

"I'll give him a call," he said.

TEN

HOLIDAY CRUSH RUSH

Stella's head spun like a top. There was so much to do before Christmas Eve. The second school was out, her mother had whisked her away to the mall. And so began their arduous process of shopping for presents.

Stella used to love shopping. What girl obsessed with fashion didn't? But the act had lost its appeal when she'd learned how to sew her own clothes and she'd realized being in the middle of huge crowds wasn't fun. The air vibrated with stress. It was supposed to be the most wonderful time of year, yet almost everyone she passed was scowling. A certain kind of frenzy and manic insanity came out of even the nicest people during the holidays.

It also didn't help that she missed her dad the most during the holidays. Actually, all of her family did. Sometimes she would still catch her mom looking at ties, socks, and polo shirts with the intent of buying them. She would play it off as if she were thinking about giving them to Cam, but Stella knew the truth. Cam even called more often. Stella suspected being away in college was messing with his being the man of the house.

What really bothered Stella was how she and Will seemed to have grown apart. She understood that school was hectic. He had final projects to submit. It cut down on his visits home. He said he needed the time to work and get things done. Stella thought she was good about being patient too. But still she sent texts, each growing sadder by the minute. "How are you?" His response was "Fine." When she sent him an "I miss you" text, all she got for a reply was a smiley-face emoji. And when all she could come up with was a sad-face meme, she got crickets. Like, nothing. She wanted to laugh and cry at the same time. It was obvious texting wasn't cutting it anymore. With things just starting out, especially after the stress of Thanksgiving, both of them being so busy was worrying her.

After a long afternoon at the mall, Stella was ready to go to bed. Her feet ached. Her arms hurt from carrying too many bags. And her stomach sloshed from the giant icee she'd allowed herself as a reward. Not even the added sugar in her system could keep her motivated to stay awake.

"Oh, you're here," she said when she entered her room and dumped her shopping bags on the floor. "Did we make plans and I forgot?"

Franklin sat cross-legged on her bed. "I guess it's safe to say that the Boyfriend Bracket is finally over?"

She glanced at the board and pouted. "Yeah. Not that Will and I are talking much these days."

"Everyone's busy. It's understandable," he said in a consoling tone. "So should we get rid of it? The board, I mean."

Stella flopped onto her bed beside him. "Nah. It's so pretty. And you worked so hard on it. Let's keep it where it is."

"I don't know if that's a compliment or not."

"It's definitely a compliment. You are the bestest friend in the world. Thank you so, so much for putting this bracket together for me." She pulled out her phone and sent a quick text to Will that she was home.

"So humor me; who would have won if the bracket continued till the end?"

Puffing her cheeks and staring at the board, she thought long and hard about the answer until her vision blurred. Then she breathed out and said, "I'd go with Joey. I liked him from the beginning."

"Yes!" Franklin threw his hands up. "I knew it. Five stars, five hearts can't be wrong!"

Her jaw dropped. "Were you taking bets or something?"

"Maybe."

She smacked his arm. He flinched away and laughed. Then he grew serious again.

"Hey, I wanted to talk to you about something before I leave for Korea," he began.

"A trip sounds nice right about now. When are you leaving?"

"Couple of days."

"Make sure to bring something cute back for me, okay?"

The small smile on Franklin's lips came and went so fast, Stella wasn't sure she'd actually seen it. "Yeah. I'll do that. Look, I wanted to ask you again about the fashion show. Are you sure you don't want to participate? It's great exposure."

"Can we not right now?" Stella rubbed her forehead. "I've been walking all day. The mall was a madhouse. And Mom was looking at socks again."

"It's about your dad, huh?"

"The holidays are still tough. That's why feeling this disconnect with Will is so depressing. I'm missing way too many people at once."

"I'm here."

From her position, she hugged him and buried her face in his side. The second she closed her eyes, all the weight she had been carrying came crashing down. She was asleep before she knew it.

THE UNFORTUNATE THING about going to bed early? Stella was awake before the sun. She crept to the kitchen and poured herself a glass of milk and made a breakfast sandwich to eat in her bedroom. Maybe she could get a jump on her winter-formal dress. The event was still over a month away, but it didn't hurt to get the initial concept on paper. She had nothing better to do.

Back in her room, she set her plate and glass on her desk. She brought half the sandwich to her lips. She was about to take a bite when her eyes wandered to her window. There was a white envelope taped to the outside.

She set the sandwich down and wiped her hands on her pajama bottoms. Giddy curiosity had her lifting the latch and pushing the pane high enough to ease her arm outside. The second her fingers closed around the envelope, she yanked it from the glass and brought it inside.

It didn't take long for her to rip it open and read its contents. At first she couldn't believe her eyes. She read the words again. The letters were in a clean, bold handwriting she would recognize anywhere. For the third pass through, she read out loud.

"Slappy, I know we've both been busy." She smiled. *"I know I haven't come home in a while. And I dropped the ball on texting you back. Can you please let me make it up to you?"* She snorted. *"The first clue is waiting at the place where you proved Cam and me wrong. Yours, Will."*

She looked out the window. Dawn was chasing away the night. She had no idea how long the envelope had been taped to her window. And she didn't know if the hunt had a time limit. Will wasn't seriously waiting for her, was he?

As if her feet had sprouted wings, Stella got dressed and ran out of the house. The holidays had given her such a solid beating these past few days that she had forgotten what a wonderful time it was. Will was in town! Her heart skipped a beat at the thought. All she had to do was go on this hunt and find him.

The first location was a no-brainer. She hurried to the playground a block away from her house. It was empty that time of morning. Only joggers were up with her. No need to think twice. She headed for the monkey bars.

There on the last rung was taped a rose and a note. She climbed up the ladder and ripped the flower and the letter from the transparent binding. Bits of tape remained on the iron bar, but Stella was too busy smelling the rose and reading the note to bother.

In Will's neat hand, it said:

Roses are red.

I made you blue.

The holidays are just around the corner,

So let me make it up to you.

The rhyme was terrible. But a smile still stretched across Stella's lips. At the bottom of the paper was the next clue. It instructed her to head to the place where double the sweetness could be found.

Easy! The diner.

The second she walked in, the waitress on duty pointed at the booth at the corner. Her booth. The one she always used.

The ancient springs creaked beneath her weight as she slid into the seat. The fried smells and aroma of fresh coffee filled her lungs. The smooth table beneath her palms featured the never-changing menu on its laminated surface.

If this was the place in the clue, Stella had no idea where to find the next one. No notes were tucked anywhere she could see. She bent down and checked underneath the table. Besides dried globs of gum, nothing clue-like caught her attention.

The waitress arrived when she sat up. She slid a tall glass

of double-chocolate milk shake in front of Stella. Along with an envelope. Dizzy excitement filled Stella's chest as she sipped the sweet goodness. She didn't care that it was six in the morning. It was never too early or late for a milk shake.

She tore into the envelope as the waitress left her table. She almost ripped the paper in half. With shaking hands, she unfolded the note. It said, *"When you're down, nothing like a double-chocolate milk shake to brighten your day."*

A blush rushed over Stella's face. It warmed her insides that Will knew about her go-to drink.

At the bottom of the page wasn't a clue. It was a single line. *"I'll be waiting for you at the place you love most in Oak Hills."*

There was only one location that matched that description. Stella finished her milk shake as fast as she could. She gritted her teeth through two brain freezes. Then she rushed to the counter to pay, but of course Will had taken care of it already. The waitress waved her off with a "Good luck."

Heart full to bursting, Stella exited the diner. She left without looking back. At the end of the block, she veered right toward the park and ran as fast as her sneakers would take her.

Will knew her. The mini scavenger hunt proved it. He knew what made her happy. He knew what gave her confidence. He knew what she loved.

Breathless, she ran into the park and followed the path that led to the center. Tall ponderosa pines stretched toward the sky. The smell of the needles filled her lungs with freshness that brought her back to life.

When she reached the picnic area with the many benches

lining the path, she stopped. Will stood in the middle of the path. He had his back to her, waiting. His hands were in his pockets. It wasn't that cold for December in Oak Hills, but a light jacket was definitely called for. Will wore his favorite one. Army-inspired camo.

Tears flooded Stella's vision at the relief that seeing him again brought. It had been weeks. She had missed him terribly. And the second he was back, he'd given her a scavenger hunt. As if he knew she needed the boost it would give. She blinked the tears away. No one was crying that day.

"Will," she said.

He turned around, and immediately a huge smile spread across his face. "Hey."

She ran. He opened his arms. She jumped into them. The second they hugged, he lifted her up and spun them around. Joyous laughter escaped her lungs, erasing all the stress, the worry, the sadness. Like a newly charged battery, Will brought her back to life.

"You're here!" she said when Will finally set her down. "You're really here."

He kissed her forehead. "I'm sorry that I couldn't come home to visit before."

She shook her head. "Nothing to be sorry for. I knew you were busy."

"I worked hard to finish everything early so I could come back here. We have the rest of the holidays together."

"Really?" She did the mental calculations. "That's almost three weeks."

"About eighteen days," Will corrected.

"Not nearly enough, but I'll take it!"

They looked into each other's eyes as if for the first time. Stella searched for him and Will searched for her in equal measure. Then she pushed to her toes and kissed him. Kissed him like she had wanted to all the weekends that he hadn't made it home. Showed him in that one kiss how happy she was that he was back.

They were both breathless when their lips finally parted.

"I'm so happy you're here," she whispered, holding onto his arms.

"There's actually something I want to ask you," he said in all seriousness.

Stella made sure she had both feet on the ground before she nodded.

Will smiled as he said, "Stella Marie Patterson, will you go to winter formal with me?"

"Really?" She couldn't believe it.

"Yeah, really." He touched his forehead against hers.

Stella felt all her emotions come up like a geyser gurgling from the depths of the earth. The tears she had been holding back finally freed themselves from her control.

"Is that a yes?" Will asked, drying her cheeks with the pads of his thumbs.

She laughed and nodded. "Yes."

ELEVEN
MISLEADING MISTLETOE

It was Christmas Eve and Will was living in the clouds. His parents had flown in for the occasion. They could stay only for the day, but he'd take all the hours they could spend together that he could get. The call to the agent had turned out to be legit. He'd put together a submission sample of the comic, and the agent had sent it out to interested editors, saying the soonest they would hear back was the second or third week of January. And, best of all, Stella was in his life. His chest was like a balloon filled with helium every time they saw each other.

The Pattersons were coming over. It was another one of their families' traditions: Christmas Eve at the Montgomerys'.

Will already had the perfect gift for Stella tucked away in his room. Actually, there were two presents. The one under the tree was a decoy to throw Cam off the scent. A pair of socks. Nothing romantic about a pair of socks. The real gift, Will would give when they got some time alone. He already had a plan in place on how to get Stella to his room without anyone noticing.

Since his parents were home for the first time in months, Nana decided to kick the party up a notch by inviting the neighborhood. The Montgomery house got crazy, with tons of food, overflowing eggnog, and all the Christmas carols available on iTunes.

The doorbell rang just as Will set down a fresh bowl of his nana's famous fruit salad on the buffet table.

"I'll get it," Will announced over the small talk and happy music. His heart beat faster the closer he got to the door, and he opened it.

Cam was the first to step forward, pulling him into a back-slapping hug. "Merry Christmas, bro."

"Merry Christmas," he returned. "It's a madhouse today."

"All's good. Now where's that fruit salad at?"

Will pointed over his shoulder. "Just put down a fresh batch."

Cam rubbed his hands together and went in search of his bounty. Will then welcomed Mrs. Patterson, giving Stella's mom a kiss on the cheek. Mrs. Patterson handed over a pie, saying it was made with young coconut—her specialty. Will thanked her with his most charming smile. He stepped aside and let her through, pointing out where he had last seen his parents.

Stella brought up the rear and stopped Will's heart in a red dress with a white bow on her collar. His eyes fell out of his skull. How lucky was he to have her in his life?

He looked over his shoulder. Only when he was sure no one was paying them any attention did he step out and wrap an arm around Stella's waist, bringing her close. He inhaled her scent.

"You're the best present in the world," he whispered into her ear. "Thank you, Santa."

"Don't think so." She lifted a wrapped box the size of a Rubik's Cube. "*This* is your gift, mister."

Smiling, he leaned in and gave her a kiss. She melted into him. The murmurs that she made were so damn hot.

Before he forgot that they were standing by the door of a packed house, Will stepped back. But not before planting another kiss. This time on the corner of her sweet, sweet lips. She giggled, blushing prettily.

"Well," she said, breathless. "A ho, ho, ho to you. Please don't tell me that was your gift."

"Nuh-uh. But if more of that is my gift, then I'll take it," Will whispered back, grinning ear to ear. And he meant every word.

"You're so easy to please." Stella scrunched her cute nose. "What am I going to do with this, then?" She indicated the box again.

"You're too good to me." He took her hand and led her inside. But as soon as the front door closed behind them, he let go, as much as he didn't want to.

"Good call," Stella said. "Too many eyes. I'll put this under the tree. Catch you later."

If Will had it his way, he'd have his arm around her the entire night, introducing her as his girlfriend to anyone who would listen. But Cam wouldn't appreciate that. As far as he knew, Will was just staying present in Stella's life so unworthy guys stayed away from her.

Pushing his conflicting emotions aside, Will headed straight for the kitchen and deposited the pie into the fridge. Soon after, he was pulled into a conversation about how he was doing in school.

NO MATTER HOW full the house, Stella always kept an eye out for Will. Once in a while their gazes met and a shock of electricity ran through her. She was so aware of him, even when they were on opposite sides of the room.

Nursing a cup of warm apple cider, she mingled. Answering questions about her future. What colleges she had applied to. Had she heard back yet? Some schools were already sending out responses.

Every time she mentioned fashion, she got one of two reactions. The first was dismayed pity, because for the people she was talking to, fashion wasn't a real career, usually followed by suggestions of alternatives like medicine or law. Or even becoming a physical therapist because someone's aunt said it was an in-demand job at the moment. The second reaction was of impressed awe and requests for clothes when she got famous. On both occasions, she just smiled until her cheeks ached.

Needing a break, Stella excused herself from the latest group to demand her attention only to bump into someone.

"Oh, sorry!" she said, immediately turning to see Will's smile. It seemed like hours since the last time they'd stood so close.

"Did you eat?" was Will's concerned question. "All I've seen you holding is that cup."

As if in response to his words, Stella's stomach growled. Even in the crowded room, her body's demand seemed so loud. They shared a chuckle.

"Now that I think about it . . ." She rubbed her belly.

The air around them stilled. It was like the calm before the starting gun of a race. Stella looked around. Will did too. It seemed like all eyes were on them.

Oh no! she thought. Had they been that obvious? Was their cover blown? Stella replayed her interaction with Will. Nothing seemed out of the ordinary. Just two friends catching up. Had she been so used to being with Will that any action looked more than innocent? Her heart sputtered. Panic quickly filled her insides.

Then someone said, "Kiss her already!"

"What?" Stella yelped.

She looked to Will for an explanation. His expression was as panicked as she felt. Her gaze picked that time to land on her brother. Cam watched them.

To add fuel to the fire, a chant began: "Kiss her. Kiss her."

Still, Stella had no clue as to why everyone wanted them to kiss until Cam pointed at the ceiling. She glanced up. Will did the same.

"Ah, crap," he said under his breath. "I completely forgot about that."

By *that*, Will meant the sprig of mistletoe looming over them. Stella's heart leaped to her throat, then just as fast plunged into the deepest depths of her stomach. Not good. So not good. How were they going to kiss and not reveal their secret?

All Will had to do was stand near Stella and her knees grew weak. A kiss? A kiss turned her to mush.

Will's hands closing around her arms pulled her away from her thoughts. Their eyes met. His gaze seemed to say everything was going to be okay. Stella didn't believe him. *Just one quick kiss*, she could see him trying to tell her silently. She would have shaken her head if it wouldn't have been too obvious.

"On three," Will whispered so softly that she almost didn't hear him.

There was no avoiding it. Her heart beat so hard, she thought she was going to pass out. Sweat covered her hands. Her skin prickled. It must have been impossible for Will not to feel Cam's gaze drilling a hole between them.

Taking a deep breath, Stella puckered her lips. As did Will. If she had been watching them, she would have been laughing her ass off. Their mouths barely grazed each other before they were flinging their bodies in opposite directions. A round of applause and laughter engulfed them. Will was whisked away by a group of guys, hassling him for the lame kiss.

Stella was pulled into an overly cheery conversation. She gave what was being said only half an ear. Her face was too hot.

And Cam was nowhere in sight. What was going through her brother's mind?

"Meet me in my room," Will said discreetly as he passed her. "Ten minutes."

Stella nodded once, keeping a fake smile on her face though her insides were in knots. Will walked away. She breathed in and out through lungs that felt like they weren't taking in air.

EXACTLY TEN MINUTES LATER, Will climbed the stairs that led to the second floor of Nana's house. He couldn't get away from the party fast enough. The look on Cam's face had bothered him. It was as if he knew too much. But maybe he was being paranoid.

At the top of the stairs, Will turned left. His room was at the end of the hallway. He swallowed. A light sweat covered the hands he'd stuffed into his pockets. The girl of his dreams was in his room. A part of him felt as nervous and unsure as a twelve-year-old going on his first date. Another part of him was excited. If he were a dog, his tail would have been wagging frantically.

Outside his room, Will paused. His hand shook as he reached for the knob. Nothing was going to happen. He just wanted to talk. Touch base about that awkward-as-hell mistletoe kiss.

He didn't know how to feel about it. Maybe Stella would have answers. He turned the knob and pushed into his room. A step in, he stopped. Stella stood at his desk, studying the panels he had been working on for the Christmas special of his comic.

His chest ached. She was so beautiful. So soft. So delicate. Yet she possessed a strength that blew him away. He couldn't breathe. His fingers itched to touch her. To comb through her hair. To glide up the curve of her back.

"Which part of the story is this?"

Her voice unstuck his legs. He shut the door and traversed the five steps that separated them. He pulled her into his arms and buried his face in her hair. She smelled of Christmas and sweetness.

Stella wrapped her arms around his waist and rested her cheek against his chest. He was sure she heard how hard his heart was beating for her. He loved how quickly she embraced him. She was his reason. For everything.

"You're extra clingy today," she teased. "Not that I'm complaining."

"What do you think?" he asked into her hair. "Did we do a good-enough acting job?"

She stilled. "I don't know. Maybe? Stupid mistletoe. That wasn't how I imagined that kiss going."

He lifted her chin with his finger and bent down. The softness of her lips welcomed him without hesitation. Without needing encouragement, she opened for him, craving the touch of his tongue as much as he did hers. He tasted the apple cider she had been nursing all night and the sweetness of peppermint.

His other hand traced the line of her back until he reached her hair. His fingers plunged greedily into the soft strands. She shifted to her toes, and he supported her weight against him. The feel of her was warmth and all things incredible.

A small voice reminded him that not three steps away was his bed. He could easily move them. But Will pushed the thought away. He didn't ask her to his room for that, no matter how much he wanted to.

Will savored a minute more of the kiss before he set Stella down. He ran his thumb below her bottom lip, taking some of her smudged lipstick with it. She reached up and traced the corners of her mouth with her fingers. A part of Will took primal pleasure in being the one responsible for smearing her lipstick. If it wouldn't raise questions, he would walk the party proud with her lipstick on his lips. The urge to kiss her again was strong. Every time they touched, it was all he wanted.

Instead, calling on all his self-control, he closed his hand around hers and kissed the center of her palm before saying, "That should have been our first mistletoe kiss."

"I can't feel my legs."

"That good, huh?"

She smacked his chest playfully before turning in his arms to face his desk. "The comic?"

He nudged them forward. "It's a side story. Morla celebrates the holidays with the fae. Hilarity ensues the second she gets drunk on fae wine."

Stella looked over her shoulder at him and frowned. "You're not going to make me do anything crazy."

She looked so adorable that he kissed the tip of her nose. "First, I love that you think of yourself as Morla. And second, nothing too embarrassing."

With a pout she demanded, "Tell me."

The imp in Will enjoyed Stella's expectant pout too much. "Like everyone else, you'll have to wait and see."

"No fair." The pout grew deeper. "Don't I have perks? Being the girlfriend of the creator and the inspiration for the main character?"

"You make a really good point." He pretended to think about it, then said, "But, no."

"You're mean!"

Will disengaged from the embrace and strode to a corner of his room. He reached behind the shelves filled to overflowing with graphic novels and produced a velvet box that fit in the palm of his hand. Stella eyed it when he returned to her side.

"I hope this makes up for the secrecy." He took her hand and placed the box in it. "Merry Christmas."

Stella flipped the lid and gasped. She pulled out a silver chain with a pendant in the shape of an hourglass with an exploding star at the center. "Is this the necklace Cyril gave Morla before he was captured and put into suspended animation?"

Will took the necklace from her. Stella turned her back on him. He undid the clasp and put the necklace on her. She closed her hand around the pendant, which rested just above her heart.

"I found this shop that does custom jobs," Will explained.

"Doesn't this symbolize Cyril's immortal love for Morla? That wherever she is, he will always find her?"

"The infinity of time and the brightness of an exploding star. We continue to see its light long after it is gone."

"That's huge, Will."

"Look, don't freak out. I don't expect anything in return." Will spread a hand over his chest. "I know what my feelings are for you, and, like Cyril, I'm willing to wait. You don't have to say or do anything. Just know that I'm for real."

Her expression softened. "Will . . ."

"Will, you up there?" Cam called from out in the hall, his footsteps getting closer.

Stella slapped a hand over her open mouth. Fear was clear in her eyes. Will quickly looked around his room. Other than jumping out of a two-story window, Stella's only option was the closet. He did a quick inventory of the stuff inside. Nothing too embarrassing for her to find.

He yanked open the door, and without prompting, Stella jumped in. Complete remorse slammed into Will. He hated having to hide Stella in such a manner. It wasn't what the girl he loved deserved. But what could he do? As soon as he turned away from his closet, his bedroom door opened.

"Did you see my sister?" Cam asked. "I think she came up here."

Not knowing what to do with his hands, Will crossed his arms. Feeling awkward, he uncrossed them, then stuffed his hands into the pockets of his jeans.

"No. No." He looked around his room, totally blowing trying to act cool. "Not here."

"You okay?" Cam stepped into his room.

Will stifled the urge to block the closet with his body. "Yeah. Yeah." He ran his fingers through his hair. Stella had her hands all over the strands earlier. Were they sticking out? Did Cam notice?

"You don't look okay." Cam studied him.

"Too many people in the house," Will blurted out, unable to think of a better excuse. "I hate parties."

Cam stared at him for a long minute. Will resisted shifting his weight. It was torture. The closet wasn't that big. And it was filled with his stuff. Stella wouldn't suffocate, he reminded himself. Although it killed him that she was in there, kicking Cam out might only make him more suspicious.

Finally, Cam blinked. His facial features took on a concerned expression Will didn't like. "I need to talk to you about something."

Seeing an opening, Will turned Cam toward the door. "Sure," he said. "Why don't we do that downstairs? I'm thirsty."

Cam quickly turned back around and sat on Will's bed instead. "It's better we talk here. It's about Stella."

Will's ears perked up. He glanced at the closet. "What about her?"

"I don't know how to say this," Cam began, then sighed. "Dude, I know that you aren't serious here, but you should be more careful around my sister."

A thump followed Cam's words.

"What was that?"

Will coughed into a fist. "Must be a rat. Been hearing things getting knocked over in the attic."

Cam looked up. "Better take care of that. Where there's one, there's always more."

"That's what I keep telling Nana." Will cleared his throat. "Are you sure you don't want to talk over apple cider?"

"This is serious, bro." Cam squeezed the back of his neck. "I saw Stella during that lame-ass mistletoe kiss. Thanks, by the way."

"For what?" Will squeaked out. A cold sweat dotted his back.

"For not taking advantage of her." Cam got to his feet. All the tension in his shoulders eased. "She used to have such a huge crush on you. We don't want to get her hopes up." He turned and walked to the door.

Will swallowed, feeling his throat close. "Of course."

"Thanks, bro. I knew I could count on you."

He bit his tongue. What Cam was basically saying was that no matter what Will did, he would never be serious about Stella. Not in her brother's eyes, anyway. Heart heavy, he glanced back at his closet before leaving his room with Cam.

ONCE STELLA HEARD the door to Will's room click shut, she counted to twenty. She figured the number was high enough that it ensured Cam and Will were long gone. That it was safe for her to leave the closet. Yet, when she reached twenty, she didn't move. She sat on a stack of shoe boxes behind Will's shirts. They all smelled like him. In fact, the entire closet smelled like him. Despite the cramped space, she was comfortable.

What Cam had said got her thinking. Until that night, she thought she'd hidden her crush on Will pretty well. Apparently, her secret-keeping skills were nonexistent since Cam knew about it. What was he thinking, warning Will away from getting her hopes up? Too late for that. Her hopes were up. *Way* up, as she closed her hand around the pendant on the necklace

Will had given her. She couldn't have asked for a better Christmas present.

But no matter how good a mood she was in, it didn't erase the fact that Cam was sniffing around. She and Will had to be extra careful moving forward. Stupid mistletoe.

TWELVE

NEW YEAR INSECURITIES

For New Year's Eve, Will and Stella decided to drive down to the beach, despite it being four hours away, to watch the fireworks. Ringing in the New Year by the ocean seemed so romantic. The perfect place to be with the girl he loved. They made their excuses and snuck away into the cool night air.

At an hour to midnight, Will laid out a blanket a few yards away from the roaring bonfire on the beach. On the other side of the blue flames caused by the salty driftwood were the revelers who wanted to dance the last night of the year away. Those who wanted a low-key celebration spread out along the sand on blankets. The fireworks would fly from a platform floating by the distant buoys.

Stella stretched out on the blanket and patted the space beside her. Not having to be invited twice, Will positioned himself by her side and pulled her close. She rested her head on his chest, splaying her hand there too. She sighed in contentment.

Will cradled the back of his head by bending his other arm. He felt the same calm, the same ease that seemed to flow out of Stella into him. Watching the vast expanse above them on a clear night, it was easy to get lost in each other's company. It was as if Will and Stella fit together in a way only the universe could be responsible for, he thought while running his fingers through her silky hair. He breathed in the salty breeze.

Yet no matter how content Will felt, his conversation with Cam over Christmas still bothered him. It led him to say, "I think Cam's right."

"Don't let him hear you," Stella responded with a snort. "His ego is big enough."

"Don't you ever wonder why he's so protective of you? Besides feeling like he needs to step in because your dad's not here anymore."

"Because all big brothers are jerks?"

Will smirked. "I'm being serious."

"And I'm not?"

He imagined Stella raising her eyebrow from her tone. The truth of their situation hit him all at once. "I hate to admit it, but you deserve better, Slappy."

"What's that supposed to mean?"

The quick defense in her voice warned Will to tread carefully. Murky waters ahead.

"Just that . . ." He sighed. "You deserve someone who can give you the world."

Stella sat up and looked down at Will, her expression matching the seriousness of their conversation. "For your information, I don't need a guy to give me the world. I can get everything I want myself. I'm the one who decides what I deserve. Don't tell Cam. I love him, but he can be so blind."

"You think so?" Will tried and failed to suppress his confusion.

"I know so." Stella raised her chin. "Cam is so busy 'protecting' me that he doesn't see that I'm more than capable of protecting myself." Then she poked Will's shoulder. "Where is this insecurity coming from? Is it because we have to hide this?" She pointed at him then herself in a back-and-forth motion.

"I'd be crazy not to want to show all the world that we're together."

"This isn't some caveman thing, is it? Because I'm telling you now, that doesn't fly with me. I want a guy who knows who he is and what he wants. A guy who can stand on his own."

Will stayed silent for the longest time. Stella waited, but it seemed like she was lost in thought. He couldn't allow her to think that the two of them being together wasn't a good thing. Not after he had liked her for years. So he reached out and cupped her cheek. She covered his hand with hers and entwined their fingers together. Her attention returned to him immediately. Will loved that about her. Even before they got together—albeit on the down low—she always had the ability to make him feel like he was the only one who mattered in that moment.

"You're a good guy, Will. You tolerate my brother for God only knows what reason." She continued when he shook his head. "You take care of Nana and always check on her even when you don't need to. And you understand that your parents are helping make the world a better place. What's not to like?"

"My good looks? My awesome personality?"

"There's that too. And the abs."

"Oh, good. Nice to know my hours in the gym are paying off."

Maintaining eye contact, she said, "Will, I know it's tough keeping this—us—from him, but I wouldn't have let us come this far if I didn't think you were worth it."

A smile tugged at Will's lips. Then he brought the back of her hand to his mouth and said, "You've got it all figured out, huh?"

Stella faked surprise. "I'm shocked it's taken you this long to fall for my charms."

He sat up and closed the fingers of his free hand around the back of her neck. He brought her closer until their lips met. Stella sank into the kiss. Will felt her soften against him.

"I've been in love with your charms for years, Slappy," he said against her lips.

She grimaced, pulling back so she could look into his eyes. "Why do you still keep calling me by that stupid nickname, then?"

He kissed the beginnings of her pout away. "It's an adorable nickname."

She rolled her beautiful eyes. The firelight danced in their deep brown depths. "I should really just break up with you. Maybe I do deserve better."

With lightning swiftness, Will shifted them so Stella was on her back. She let out an *oof* of surprise, blinking up at him. He hovered over her, holding both her wrists above her head.

"Not going to happen," he said, challenge clear in his tone. "You're stuck with me, Slappy. Better get used to it."

He saw the shimmer in her eyes, like she wanted to melt, but somehow she managed to maintain a straight face when she said, "Now that's the guy I fell in like with."

With heat in her eyes that called to a deep longing in him, Will bent down and finished the kiss he had started. The New Year came and went with them in each other's arms. The beauty of the explosions in the sky was largely ignored for the moment they spent forging a deeper connection between their hearts.

THIRTEEN
ALL THE FORMALITIES

Stella closed her hand around the bursting star pendant on her neck and studied the dress form. Winter formal was a few days away, and something about her dress bothered her. The draped bodice looked fine. She'd properly executed the one shoulder. She had hand sewn every gray peacock feather onto the high-low skirt. It might have been her best work yet. But something was off. And she couldn't put her finger on it.

"It's not silver enough," said Franklin from her bed. Arms crossed. Legs crossed.

"You don't get to critique after abandoning me for the holidays," she said, without taking her eyes off the dress.

"My mom wanted me to explore my roots. And that means Christmas in Korea."

"Where is my something cute?"

"Oh, as if I would forget." Franklin produced a wrapped present from his messenger bag and placed it on her bed. "Open it later." Then he sighed like a drama queen. "Being with family was annoying half the time. Everyone kept feeding me. I have a figure to maintain, after all. The only good thing that came out of that vacay was my being scouted for a K-pop group."

Stella chuckled. "Of course you'd be scouted. But I can't imagine you singing and dancing in front of adoring fans."

"That's what I told the scout. I would rather dress the singers than be one." Franklin waved a hand toward her. "Speaking of dress, yours looks like a cross between Grecian goddess and Vegas showgirl."

"Ouch!"

"That's not necessarily a bad thing." Franklin unfolded himself off the bed and stood by her side, observing the dress along with her. "I think it's the skirt."

"Too many feathers?"

"Girl, there can't be too many feathers. If you ask me, there aren't enough. If you're going there, then *go* there." Franklin circled the dress form. "It's the high-low hem throwing me off. That trend is over."

Stella's eyebrows came together. "You don't think the skirt will be too busy if I make it full-on feathers?"

"No. Then again, that's just me. You know how I love myself a bit of drama."

"A bit?"

"Okay, a lot."

Grabbing the basket of feathers from beside her desk, Stella got down on her knees and held up a bunch in front of the skirt. She tilted her head and considered. Franklin took the feathers from her and motioned for her to stand and step back.

From a different perspective, the skirt did look better without the shorter front. A part of her was annoyed that she hadn't noticed it sooner. The other part was thankful for Franklin.

"Help me sew these on?" she pleaded.

Franklin smiled in a way any K-pop artist would be proud of. "I thought you'd never ask."

ON THE MORNING of winter formal, Stella received a text from Will saying he was on his way from UCLA. He would pick her up for the dance that night. Her heart skipped. She was so excited to see him and tell him how proud she was of him. A week before, he had texted her the good news. Three editors wanted *Morla*, enough to go into an auction. She had no idea what that meant, but it sounded really important.

She was happy and nervous for him. He was gaining recognition. And he should be. The comic was fantastic. She didn't think so just because the main character was based on her. Her pride came from a place of actual admiration. Even her life was on track. Soon she would be hearing from the colleges she had applied to. Then it was *Project Runway*, baby. Everything was perfect.

Feeling buoyant and hopeful, Stella spent most of the day getting ready. With Franklin's help, her dress was more beautiful than ever. She couldn't wait to walk into that gym and show off her work.

"Stella," her mother called from downstairs. "You have mail."

Those three words sent her heart slamming against the walls of her chest. She rarely received mail. It could mean only one thing.

In her robe and with curlers in her hair, Stella rushed downstairs, taking the steps two at a time. That day's mail was on the side table. By the front door. With shaking fingers, she sorted through the stack until an envelope with the words *Parsons School of Design* caught her eye.

THE SECOND WILL was done with his last class, he hopped into his truck and was on his way to Oak Hills. To Stella. He wanted to see her beautiful face. Hear her voice in person. No more calls. No more texts. He was eager to be in her orbit again. He wanted to tell her about the results of the auction. The comic he had been painstakingly working on was being published by DC Comics under their Vertigo imprint. The same company that had brought *Sandman* to the world. It was official. He was several degrees of separation away from Neil Gaiman.

He had never allowed himself to dream of the possibility. Now it was on the table. *Surreal* was the best word to describe his current situation.

But when Will was an hour out of town, he pushed aside his desire to head straight for Stella's house. She was probably busy getting ready. He needed to do the same. If he saw her now, there was no way he was leaving her side. She wouldn't appreciate going to winter formal while he was still in his jeans and T-shirt.

He checked his phone and sent Stella a quick reply about picking her up. There was also a text from Franklin reminding him to pick up a bouquet. It was a nice change from a typical corsage, the boy with a neon streak in his hair said. Who was Will to disagree? Smiling, he silently thanked Franklin's quick thinking.

Before he left for UCLA after holiday break, he had asked Stella about her dress. She'd refused to show it to him. No matter how he poked. Prodded. Begged. She stayed firm. She even kept the color to herself.

He suspected she wanted for it to be a surprise. But, like any good boyfriend, he had to match his tie to her dress. It was part of the code. The boyfriend code. So Will took matters into his own hands. Realizing he didn't have Franklin's number, he'd asked around until someone eventually texted it to him. Best friends knew all the info. Thank God he had given Will points for going the extra mile and cooperated with minimal hostility. Franklin was on Stella's side, of course. As he should be. Will appreciated that someone had her back.

Time couldn't move fast enough for Will once he was done showering and getting dressed. The instant his clock said he could pick her up, he hurried to his truck as if a mob of bulls were after him. He had to keep reminding himself to follow traffic rules. Getting pulled over wasn't in the plan. In fact, he had to make a mental note to chill. Seeing her without immediately taking her into his arms was going to be a challenge. Not in front of her mom. And Cam's watchful eye would be on them.

Will took a deep breath after he parked his truck at the curb. He eased the mix of a dozen white and red roses the clerk had lovingly wrapped for him from the passenger seat. It was all he could do not to run to the Pattersons' front door. He stifled the urge by counting his steps. Ten in all from sidewalk to doorbell. He pushed the button. A pleasant tinkling rang out. The beautiful sound was the perfect opposite of Mrs. Patterson's worried expression when she opened the door.

"What's wrong?" Will asked immediately.

Stella's mother waved him in. "I cannot find her."

"Who?"

"I went to check on Stella, and she was not in her room" came the stream of words filled with distress. Her accent thickened. Her vowels lengthened and her consonants rounded. "She is not in the house."

Will placed the flowers on the side table by the door. His mind ran a mile a minute, going from one scenario to the next. He focused on breathing despite his heart beating in his ears. Nothing good came from panicking. It was clear his rising worry wasn't what Mrs. Patterson needed. No more fuel for the fire.

He steered her to the couch and helped her sit down. He took the cushion directly beside hers. She wrung her hands. The worry lines on her forehead deepened.

"When was the last time you saw her?" he asked, recalling all the *CSI*s he had watched. He imagined himself as Gil Grissom, without a beard and the eccentricities. "Was she upset? Was she doing anything that would lead you to believe she would leave the house suddenly?"

"I brought her a sandwich for lunch." She wore a faraway look on her face. "Stella was busy putting curlers in her hair. Then I went downstairs. I did some laundry. Then mail arrived. I called Stella, saying something came for her."

A text from a couple days ago popped into Will's mind. "Was it a college letter?"

"I think so."

Stella had casually mentioned she would start hearing back from the fashion schools she had applied to. He pushed off the couch and sent a quick SOS text to Franklin to come to Stella's house.

"Where are you going?"

He paused on the way to the kitchen. "Going to check the tree house. Everything is going to be okay."

From the back door, he pushed out into the yard and jogged toward the tree house. A series of sniffs and hiccups reached him as soon as he held on to the rung of the makeshift ladder. His heart jumped. Stella was in the tree house. She was okay. In the physical sense. At least, Will hoped so.

He made quick work of the ladder like a nimble spider monkey in dress shoes. When he poked his head through the entrance cut out of the floor, he was greeted by Stella. His chest ached.

She was sprawled in the farthest corner. The tie of her silk robe was undone. Inside she had on something equally silky and way too sexy. Totally not the right time or place to be thinking those kind of thoughts. He forced himself to focus.

Some of the curlers in her hair had come lose, scattered at her feet. Tendrils of hair fell around her face. Black streaks painted her crumpled face. Her cheeks were flushed. Her lipstick was smudged. The back of her hand had a pink smear on it. In her other hand was a piece of paper. The culprit of her heartache. Will had never been so mad at a single letter before. But he pushed aside the emotion. Stella needed him as levelheaded as possible.

He eased himself all the way into the tree house. With his bulk, he prayed they wouldn't plummet to the ground. Two people made the space seem cramped, when once it used to fit all three of them comfortably.

As if noticing him for the first time, Stella dropped the paper and covered her face with both hands. "Don't look at me!" she shrieked. "I'm hideous right now."

Will scanned the letter, confirming what he had suspected. Then he sat beside Stella. He picked her up and settled her on his lap. She squeaked but didn't move to get away. She buried her face into his chest. A new wave of tears rocked her body. Heart breaking, Will wrapped his arms around her.

"Parsons sucks," he mumbled into her hair as he rubbed circles down her back.

"They are one of the best fashion schools in the country," Stella defended. "Donna Karan is from there. So are Marc Jacobs and Anna Sui and Tom Ford and—" Her hiccups kept her from continuing.

None of those names made any sense to Will. All he knew about fashion was the Gap, where Nana bought him shirts for his birthday. He was about to respond when Stella found her second wind.

"If Parsons doesn't want me . . ." A series of sniffs and shaking sobs followed her words until she managed to say, "The rest won't want me either."

"That's not true."

The statement was meant to be comforting. It had the opposite effect. Stella pushed away enough to glare at him.

"How can you be so sure, huh?" she challenged.

Normally, he would have asked how she could be so sure too. But Will's self-preservation instincts were strong. Stella was hurt. She was like a cornered, wounded creature right now, and his chances of being bitten were astronomical. Keeping his expression neutral, Will shook his head.

"See!" Stella poked his chest hard enough for him to wince. "You're not sure."

"There has to be another way," he offered.

For a minute, a faraway look entered Stella's face. Then she said, "There's this fashion show. Franklin showed me the flyer."

As if recharged, Stella scrambled out of his lap and crawled to the entrance. In her haste, her robe opened wider, baring a shoulder. She practically jumped to the ground. Will had to widen his stride just to catch up with her.

Stella ran into the house, past her mother. She went straight up the stairs to the second floor. Will had never seen her move so fast. He assured Mrs. Patterson everything was okay, even if he didn't quite believe himself, before he followed Stella.

Without thinking if she wanted him there, he went into her room. The walls were covered with sketches for dresses and pages from magazines. One corner housed her sewing machine. The table in another was laden with fabric and more sketches. Opposite was her unmade bed. Then his gaze landed on a board made of all things that shined and sparkled. It was propped on an easel and contained eight names he recognized from Stella's book.

"Whoa!" he said, wide-eyed. "Is that the Boyfriend Bracket?" He shook his head and forced himself to focus. This wasn't the time or place.

At the center was a torso with a beautiful silver dress with what looked like a million feathers for a skirt. All he had to do was imagine Stella wearing it, and the image took Will's breath away. But she made no move to put the dress on. Instead, she was holding a piece of paper. She handed it to him.

"This is my only chance," she said, removing the last of the curlers from her hair and letting them fall to the floor.

"A fashion show?" Will asked.

"Not just any fashion show." She flipped her hair. "It's a design competition. That's my only hope. I've got to get to work."

"What about the winter formal?"

"We're not going. I need to start sketching if I want to win that scholarship to FIDM."

"Surely one night—"

"That flyer was posted last September," she cut him off like sharp scissors.

"It's not until the end of March."

"My competition's already had months to prepare. Final applications for entries are due next week." Stella was frantic and Will felt helpless. He had no idea what to say or do to make things better.

"I'll take it from here," Franklin said from behind him, striding in like he owned the place. His yellow suit screamed.

"But—"

Franklin faced Will and ushered him out the door. "You can't get through to her when she's like this. It's the sequins debacle all over again. Just go home."

Will had no idea what the sequins debacle was, but it sounded serious.

"But," he repeated, even though he had nothing else he knew to say.

"Will, go home." Franklin looked him in the eye. Behind him, Stella was already sitting at her desk, pencil flying over a piece of paper. "I promise to have her text you when she's calmed down."

Feeling lost, Will nodded. Franklin closed the door to Stella's room. The click of the lock seemed so loud in the silent hallway. Defeated, Will turned and left.

FOURTEEN

FASHIONABLY JUST IN TIME

Stella breathed a sigh of relief. All her entry requirements for the contest were submitted. She had made it before the deadline! All week, ever since the night of the winter formal, she had been vibrating with uncertainty. It was an odd, unsettling feeling. She had always been so sure of her path in life. She had been preparing for fashion school for years. To be denied entry into one of the most prestigious schools in the country was a huge blow that knocked her down.

But her determination was stronger than any rejection letter. Like the phoenix from the ashes, she would rise better than ever. She had to. It was the vow she had made to herself. She had a little over two months to come up with a dress that would blow the audience away and scoop up their votes come runway day.

Saturday morning came sooner than she expected, having been lights-out almost as soon as her head had hit the pillow the night before. She rolled over to her side, away from the beam of sunlight streaming in from her window. She had work to do, but her bed was so warm. Her hand brushed against a smooth rectangle by her pillow.

Picking up her phone, she opened one eye. Beside the time, which was five minutes after nine, was the message icon. She had received a text. She punched in her code.

Her heart squeezed. It was from Will. Of course it was. She had been the worst secret girlfriend in the world. While usually her in-box was full of their conversations, that week she had replied to him only once or twice. Sometimes with just an emoji.

So much had been happening. She caught herself wishing their relationship wasn't so secret. Sneaking around took such effort. It was exhausting. Stella ignored the text and called Will instead. Shifting flat on her back, she brought the receiver to her ear. She massaged her forehead with her other hand. After three rings, Will answered.

"Hey," he said, sounding genuinely surprised. And happy.

His cheerful tone almost made Stella waver. Almost.

"Hey," she answered, more subdued.

"How did it go?"

It was a repeat of his text. He was being supportive. It killed her how perfect he was. And here she was, imperfect. The braids, braces, and glasses might be gone, but in many ways, she was still that same girl.

"Got all the requirements in."

A breath of relief preceded the words, "That's great. I was on the edge of my seat all day."

She could hear the smile in his voice. "It would have been better if you were there when I was submitting all the requirements."

"I'm sorry," he said. "I couldn't get away. Cam was with me and—"

Stella closed her eyes and prayed for strength. "I know, I know. It's always the same when my brother's around. I'm just saying it would have been nice, that's all."

A pause followed. Then, "I'm really sorry. I don't know what to do."

Will's enthusiasm had gone down a peg. Stella hated it. She wanted him happy. She wanted him, period.

"I'm sorry," she said, the corners of her eyes growing damp. "The stress is getting to me, that's all. I wanted my boyfriend to be there."

"I should have been." His tone was as if he were tired. "Here you are taking your future seriously, and I couldn't even show my support. I'm sorry for being such a coward."

"No!" She sat up. "You're not being a coward. I'm in this too."

"I really want to see you, but I'm swamped here." The worst part was the helplessness in his voice.

Stella shook her head, even if Will couldn't see the action.

"No." She closed her hand around the pendant. "I completely understand. I have to work on the dress for the fashion show, so even if you came I won't be able to hang out."

There was a long silence that followed. At one point, Stella thought Will had hung up on her. But when she checked her phone's screen, the call was still in progress. So she waited.

Finally, just when she was about to speak again, a long breath came from Will's end. She imagined him running his ink-stained fingers through his hair. When he spoke again, Stella thought she couldn't be more heartbroken than she already was.

"We're okay. Right? Please tell me we're okay?"

She gasped, unsure why his logic went in that direction. "Of course we're okay," she said with conviction. "Just busy."

"Like before the holidays."

"Yeah." Her heart sputtered. "But we'll text more."

"We will."

But when she ended the call, she got the feeling she wasn't telling the truth.

"You didn't have to do that," Franklin said from the left side of her bed. He had spent the night. "You guys can hang out."

Stella frowned. "I need to put all the time I have left into this."

"Girl, that boy is the kind of distraction you need to keep you focused."

"I thought this year was just going to be about dances and waiting for acceptance letters." Her shoulders slumped. "But it's not looking like that anymore."

"You crazy."

"I'm being practical. Will's doing his thing. I need to do mine. And that means banging out a rocking dress for this competition."

"I can help."

Stella straightened. "You have your own design to worry about."

"I'm months ahead of you." Even without product in his hair and sans makeup, Franklin still looked stunning. Stella resented his flawless complexion for a second.

"But you're not done," she insisted.

Franklin sat up and stretched like a cat in a patch of sunlight. "I can withdraw from the competition."

"Nuh-uh." Stella shoved a finger toward his porcelain-skinned face. "Just because you got into Parsons doesn't mean you can coast."

"I'm sorry." But it didn't look like he was, though.

Stella placed her hands on his shoulders and shook him gently. Franklin's head bobbed as if he were a bobblehead.

"It's not your fault. Parsons just didn't like my portfolio." She was proud that not a hint of bitterness tainted her voice. "You motivate me. You're my competition. I'm taking you down."

The glint in his eye told her the taunt had worked. "Then prepare to lose."

"Over my fashionably dressed dead body." She returned his smile of challenge. "That scholarship is mine. Now I'm taking a shower, and we're having breakfast; then we'll start work on the dress."

"Sounds like a plan." Franklin powered his own phone and was fiddling with the screen while Stella crawled out of bed and put together the clothes she was wearing that day.

"Holy crap!"

"What?" Stella looked toward Franklin. He was slack-jawed, staring at his phone. "What is it?"

He showed her the screen. She was too far to see properly, so she stormed the five steps from her closet to her bed and took the phone from him. The screen featured an online article.

"That idiot," she said, a smile stretching her lips.

"He didn't tell you?"

She shook her head, making up her mind. "You and I are going for a drive. I'm going to knock some sense into this fool; then we're going fabric shopping at Mood."

Franklin mirrored her grin. "I like that plan even better."

EVERY FEW MINUTES, Will looked up from the panel he was inking to stare at his phone. He hated how the call with Stella had ended. He should have gotten into his truck and driven to Oak Hills to see her. But he was on a deadline too. One she didn't know about. How could he have told her when she was under so much stress?

He figured while she was busy with the dress, he would put his head down, incorporate the notes about the comic from his editor, send the entire thing in, and then worry about repairing his relationship with Stella. And that started with planning on how to tell Cam. With the release coming in eight months, he was going to find out anyway, and that scared the shit out of Will. It would be infinitely better if Cam heard from the horse's mouth.

His mind was made up. He had to keep working.

The tip of his ink pen was about to make contact with Morla's thigh when the door to his dorm slammed open. He startled with a yelp. The pen flew away from his desk to land on his bed, leaking onto his sheets. An inkblot started to form. He turned to face whoever had surprised him—and not in a good way—with choice expletives ready to leave his mouth. But all the words disappeared when he recognized who was standing by his door like an avenging angel.

"Stella? What are you doing here?" he blurted out, eyes about to fall out of their sockets.

Instead of responding, she pulled out her phone and showed him the screen. "Why didn't you tell me?"

And there it was. An article announcing the deal he'd inked with Vertigo. It detailed everything, including the expedited release schedule. Thank God Cam wasn't into social media of any kind, or Will and Stella would have been in a world of trouble.

"This article came out a day after winter formal," she said before he could say anything. "That means you knew even before then. Right?"

There was genuine sadness in her eyes. He wiped his hand down his face, leaving an ink streak on his cheek. "I was going to tell you during the dance, but . . ."

"We never went to the dance," she finished for him.

"And you were upset about Parsons. I thought that was the absolute worst time to tell you."

She ran to him, got on her knees, and threw her arms around his shoulders. "It would have been the absolute right time to tell me, you idiot."

"What?" He looked into her eyes. What he had mistaken as tears of sadness at first were actually tears of joy. "You would have been happy for me?"

"I would have been so happy for you." She kissed him. Then pulled back just as quick. "I'm totally happy for you. This is it, Will."

He was in awe of her. If there was a time he thought he couldn't love her more, it was that moment. "You drove all this way. . . ."

"Just to knock some sense back into you." She held his head between her hands. "No matter what I'm going through, don't you ever keep something this huge from me again. Or I will never forgive you!"

He nodded as best he could while she held him. "I promise."

They kissed for the longest time. Only fear of Cam walking in on them brought them to their senses. Stella and Will got to their feet, holding hands.

"So we'll both be busy for a while, huh?" she said with a bit of longing in her tone.

"But it's a good kind of busy." He kissed the tip of her nose. "Why don't we set up a time each night where we can talk? No distractions."

She smiled, dazzlingly bright. "I like that."

He squeezed her hand. "Are you headed back to Oak Hills? We can have lunch first."

"Franklin's with me." She gestured toward the door. "He's waiting in the parking lot. We plan on heading to fabric stores after here."

"I see. There was a hidden agenda to your good intentions," he teased.

"You do have the best fabric stores here. I'd be dumb not to take advantage of that." She must have seen through his brave face because she added, "But I can definitely squeeze in lunch. Something off campus, of course."

His chest swelled. All was right between them again. It was exactly what Will needed. Now he felt like he could work and everything would be okay.

FIFTEEN

SINGLES AWARENESS DAY

The freaking dress was not cooperating! The bodice was all wrong. The skirt was hideous. Who was she to think fuchsia was an awesome color choice? And silk? Was she completely insane? She might as well be working with neoprene.

Franklin was off putting the finishing touches on his dress, and she hadn't seen or heard from him in a week. Which was frustrating, because she wanted to bounce her idea off someone, but her usual sounding board was also hard at work.

The only thing keeping her mostly sane was her nightly call with Will. Between nine and ten p.m. every day, she was able to breathe again. They hadn't seen each other since she'd dropped in unannounced at his dorm room. She missed him terribly and told him so every time they spoke. He too was hard at work on the edits for *Morla*. Although what he still needed to fix was beyond her. The comic was perfect in her eyes. She wished she could say the same about the stupid dress.

Stella yanked the incomplete garment off the dress form and flung it over her shoulder. It was the second dress she had rejected. Tim Gunn's voice in her head kept saying it wasn't working. The combination was terrible. The construction work shoddy. And that she was running out of time. His buttery accent didn't make the truth any less real.

All around her room were scraps of fabric and drawings of dresses. None of them were good enough. Big enough. Grand enough. Worth a scholarship to FIDM. She needed a *pow*! A knock-their-socks-off moment on that UCLA runway. But inspiration was being fickle. This was a first for her. Usually, the first dress that popped into her mind's eye was the one.

Shoving her hands into her hair, she closed her fingers around the strands and pulled. Even the prickling pain on her scalp wasn't working. She turned. And paused. The dress she had discarded had landed on Will's head and shoulders. Apparently he had been in the process of entering her room at the time she'd thrown the silk monstrosity over her shoulder. His hand was still on the knob.

A giggle burst out of her. She covered her mouth with both hands. Her shoulders shook from the effort of trying not to throw her head back and laugh. Will reached up with his free hand and pulled the dress off his head. He wore a rueful smile on his lips. Then he said, "Hey, Slappy. Guess this one didn't make the cut?"

All the mirth in Stella vanished like a morning mist. No matter how much she wanted to leap into his arms, the reality of her situation kept her from doing so. She rubbed her face, then slapped her cheeks. Maybe she needed coffee. Or an energy drink. Or both mixed together. Yeah, that was it.

"Look, I love you being here," she said, her eyes darting from one rejected sketch to the next. "But you have to go."

"Happy Valentine's Day."

She froze. "What?"

When she looked back at Will, he had a rose in his hand. Red. Single stem. Like the one he had left her on the playground. Had he tucked it away in his back pocket or something? Because he sure hadn't been holding it when he had come into her room.

He handed the beautiful bloom to her. "It looks like you need a break."

She accepted the rose and brought it to her lips. She inhaled its heady perfume. The velveteen petals tickled her lips.

"I don't have time," she whispered.

"I'll go if that's what you really want," Will said, tilting his head toward the door.

The word *no* hovered at the tip of Stella's tongue. It was so good to see him. His handsome face. And hearing the sound of his voice IRL. He was the sun, and she was the sunflower needing his light. His warmth.

"What about your edits?"

"Done." He clapped his hands once. "All done."

"Really?" A wide smile transformed her face. "Oh, Will! Congratulations!"

"It's just the first round. I'm waiting to see if there's a second one."

"But you're done!" She was so happy for him. Now if she could only be happy for herself, that would be swell.

"It really looks like what you need is a break," Will insisted. "Grab your stuff. I have something to show you."

Stella didn't move at first. Half of her said she had to stay. She needed to start a new sketch. Maybe another trip to the fabric store. The other half reminded her it was Valentine's Day. How could she have forgotten? And Will was here. He'd driven three hours to see her. Will. Her perfect Will.

Missing him won over her need to work. It was what pushed Stella into action. It wasn't like she was getting anything done anyway. Might as well spend the rest of the day with him.

AN HOUR LATER, Stella was surrounded by the most glamorous dresses in fashion history.

"I had dinner plans, but I decided the *Icons of Fashion* exhibit was a good pit stop along the way," Will said, spreading his arms wide.

They were the only ones at the museum. The rest of the world filled restaurants and movie theaters. Stella wasn't hungry anyway. Fashion fed her. Recharged her.

"Will," she breathed out. Her eyes jumped from one dress to the next.

There were gowns from all the big names in fashion. Her eyes feasted on the myriad fabrics, ranging from classic to avant-garde designs. She stood in front of a black Valentino gown with white piping detailing and a tulle train.

"This is the dress Julia Roberts wore when she won the Best Actress Oscar," she said, in awe of the simple yet elegant design.

"How do you know that?" Will asked, coming to stand beside her.

"My mom watches the Oscars for the stars. I watch for the fashion. Even the shows from earlier years are on YouTube." She moved to the next dress. The name plate read JACQUE-LINE DURRAN. "This one Keira Knightley wore in the movie *Atonement*. The awesome thing about it is that the designer took elements of the twenties and the thirties to make the dress, even if the movie was set in the thirties and forties."

"I like the color," Will said simply.

"You can never go wrong with emerald-green silk." Stella sighed, basking in the dress's beauty. "And this one," she pointed to the next. "Halle Berry wore to the 2002 Oscars. Burgundy taffeta skirt with an embroidered net top. It's daring yet sophisticated."

"You really know a lot about this stuff." The awe in Will's voice was unmistakable.

"Fashion is my life," she said, the ache in her voice all too real. "We live in fashion. I feel like I'm nothing without it."

"Don't say that."

"But it's true." She turned in a tight circle. "Just look at this room. All these beautiful dresses. I need this in my life, Will. I need it like my lungs need air. One day one of my dresses will be in a room like this, showing a girl with a dream that she too can make art and have someone wear it."

Then her eyes landed on the most magnificent dress of all. It took up so much space, it practically engulfed the mannequin it was on. The spotlight above it shined so bright.

"That's it." Stella ran to the dress. Will followed in her wake. "This is the kind of dress I need to make."

"It's huge."

"It's the dress Carrie wore the night she was waiting for Petrovsky in Paris." At his blank expression, she added, "When we were in eighth grade, Franklin and I used to sneak episodes of *Sex and the City*. We watched that show for the fashion. This dress is Versace. A *Cosmo* editor described it as acres and acres of tulle and chiffon in a darkly romantic color. The kind of dress that takes you out of reality. The kind of dress that makes the world a better place just by being in it."

As if a light bulb went on in her mind, Stella saw, clear as day, the dress she needed to make. She had to sketch it right away. But before that, she threw herself into Will's arms. It took him a second to understand what was happening before he reacted.

She wrapped her arms around his neck and pulled him down for a kiss. Her toes curled at the sweetness of it. Then, like the darkest chocolate, it turned rich and lush. Will pulled her against him like a man starved. She fell into the kiss, fed off it. Needing the power of its magic.

"Does this mean it's back to leaving you alone?" Will asked after he'd set her back on unsteady feet.

She cradled his sad face in her hands and looked him in the eye. "First, you're taking me to the fabric store."

His eyebrow went up. "I am?"

She nodded. "Then you're taking me to dinner."

"Really now?"

"Then you're taking me home and helping me with this dress."

"Only if you ask nicely." But the smile on his lips was unmistakable.

"I'm going to need all the help I can get. Get ready to sew like your life depends on it."

His grin grew wider. "I like the sound of that."

Stella shifted to her toes until her forehead pressed against his. "Real talk?"

"Yeah."

"I was scared."

"Of what?"

"Of not becoming successful at my own thing."

"That's crazy."

"I never said I was sane." She shifted back on her feet so their gazes locked. "I wanted to show you and the world that I can do this."

Silence wrapped around them like a wool blanket. Stella waited for what Will was about to say. His expression grew serious.

"Then we've got a ton of work to do," he said.

The statement was better than any encouragement he could have given her. It drove her to say, "I think I'm falling in love with you."

Will gave her a lopsided grin. "Best Valentine's Day ever."

"Shut up!"

"I did good?"

"You did good."

SIXTEEN
SPRING NOT-SO-BREAK

Will hissed as the needle made friends with his finger. A drop of blood leaked out of the punctured skin. He quickly put the tip into his mouth to keep from staining the giant dress in front of him.

"Again?" Franklin asked, exasperated.

"I'll get the kit," Stella said, walking out of her room.

"It's the last one without a Band-Aid." Will studied his finger. "I was going for symmetry."

"Well, congratulations." Stella strode back in and kneeled before him. The compassionate smile on her pretty face slayed him. She took his hand in hers and said, "Thank you. You didn't have to spend your spring break sewing a million beads into this monstrosity."

He kissed the tip of her nose. "You look hot in your glasses."

Stella adjusted the black frames. A blush covered her cheeks.

"More sewing, less flirting," Franklin admonished.

Will leaned back on his other hand. He had been sitting on the floor of Stella's room since he'd got back that morning. The sun had since gone from yellow to orange. He hadn't moved an inch.

"Franklin's right," he said while Stella wrapped a bandage around his last un-pricked finger.

"I'm always right," the neon-haired Korean confirmed.

Will and Stella both rolled their eyes.

"It's going to be an awesome dress." Will looked up at the voluminous confection.

"I'm not even done with the top half." Stella placed a kiss on Will's finger, then pushed to her feet. "Boning a corset isn't easy. Especially with this new technique I'm trying. The audience won't see it—"

"But it's worth it." Franklin's needle flew in and out of the fabric on his side of the skirt so fast, his hand was a blur.

"How are you so good at that?" Will asked, truly impressed.

"Practice," Stella and Franklin answered like twins.

"Remember that time we were learning how to sew sequins on a dress?" Stella asked, returning to her side of the skirt.

"Mine was so crooked, I practically invented my own design." Franklin cut the thread, knotted the end, picked up a bead, and started a new section. "This floral design is divine."

"I was inspired by the rose Will gave me on Valentine's Day." Stella winked at Will.

"Gag me." Franklin actually gagged. "I take it back."

Unfazed, Stella said, "Thank you for helping me."

"I'm here for you."

"Me too," Will piped in, feeling left out.

"More sewing!" Stella and Franklin barked at him.

BY MIDNIGHT, Stella had called it a day and sent everyone home. When even she and Franklin were pricking their fingers, it was a clear sign to stop. The last thing she wanted was traces of their DNA on the dress before it walked the runway. Exhausting herself and those helping her wouldn't get the dress done any faster.

Will left through the front door but came back through her window.

"What are you doing?" Stella whisper-hissed, even if she was happy that he was in her room again.

Will shrugged. It was like the earth moved when his shoulders did. "Wasn't ready to say good night yet."

Stella had no argument for that. Instead she climbed under the covers of her bed—the only area free of clutter—and patted the space beside her.

"You sure?"

"Cuddling," she said, serious as a heart attack.

His features softened. "Cuddling."

It wasn't like Stella hadn't thought about doing it with Will.

She'd caught herself daydreaming on more than one occasion, wondering what it would be like. She just wasn't ready.

She shifted to her side, fitting her back against his front. He gathered her into his arms, pulling her close. He nuzzled the back of her head.

"I'm addicted to your shampoo," he said, voice muffled by her hair.

Giggles came out of her like champagne bubbles. "You like coconut. Noted."

"That pie your mom makes . . ."

"*Buko* pie. Apparently, it's famous in the Philippines."

"Have you ever been?"

"I plan to. My aunt and uncle still live there. I was thinking the summer before college. But now, with everything so up in the air . . . I don't know."

Will nudged her. "Don't think like that. You'll get in."

"I won't hear back from the others until after the competition," she said with a sigh.

"Then we'll focus on the dress for now."

"Why are you so good to me?"

"Because you're easy to be good to."

"How do you do that?"

"What?" he asked.

"Stay positive all the time. Even with Cam, you always seem to have the answers. Like nothing ever bothers you."

"I don't always feel that way."

"Oh?"

There was a pause. It was heavy and thick. Like Will was

gathering up the courage to tell her something. When the words came, they were enough to push Stella into a seated position.

"We need to tell Cam."

"What?" Her eyebrows climbed up to her hairline. "Where's this coming from?"

Will pulled her back down. This time she was facing him. A blush crept across her cheeks. The position seemed so intimate. There was barely any room between them. He was so close, she could kiss his neck and jaw and chest. If she wanted to. She was tempted. Oh, she was tempted.

"Hear me out," Will said, breaking her thoughts. "I know we agreed we had to keep this from him."

"I'm not ready for that" was her response, worried. "I'm not ready to lose you."

"Who says you'll lose me?"

"I know Cam. I know how he'll react."

"But the longer we keep this from him—"

"I'd keep it from him forever if it means I get to keep you."

Will stood his ground. "He needs to know. I'm tired of lying to him and keeping you a secret. I want the world to know I'm with the best girlfriend anyone could want."

Her pout turned into a sunshine smile. "Flattering me won't work."

"Yeah?" He poked her side and she squirmed.

Stella forced herself to focus on the conversation. "What changed?"

"I'm serious about you."

"Will? What are you saying?"

"There's no cure for loving you." He breathed her in. "I can't bring myself to think about being with anyone else. Look, I get it. You need time. I can wait as long as you want. But I want you to know that this—you—are it for me. My heart is about to be published for the world to see, and I want you by my side when that finally happens."

There was too much to process all at once. Stella found herself blinking and speechless. For a long moment, all she could hear was the rhythmic beating of her heart. And if she concentrated hard enough, she was sure she could hear Will's heart calling to hers too.

What was stopping her from responding? She had liked him long before he had started liking her. What was she afraid of? This was it. All she wanted.

Yet the question "Are you sure?" still came out of her lips. But before Will could speak, she clarified, "I'm serious about you too."

"Then what's the problem?"

"Are you sure you're willing to lose Cam? Because we both know he's not going to like this."

"Who says he will go ballistic? You never know. If we come clean, maybe he'll support us."

"There you go, being Mr. Positive again." It was what she liked about him. To Will, even a rainy day was a good thing.

"Cam will just have to understand my feelings for you. I'm not going anywhere."

The declaration shouldn't have caught Stella off guard, but it did. Her stomach flipped like a pancake. *Is this really happening?* she asked herself, burying her hot face against Will's chest. She inhaled his scent. Soap on skin. Clean and slightly salty. No aftershave this time.

"What's wrong?" Will rubbed circles down her back.

"I'm so happy right now, I don't know how I'm going to get any sleep."

Will chuckled. She felt the vibrations against her cheek. "So we're telling him."

She eased back to look up at his face. "We're telling him."

They shared a smile. Then a kiss. Then they were full-on making out. But it didn't last long. They must have been more tired than Stella first thought because soon enough, they were fast asleep in each other's arms.

"WHAT THE FUCK is going on here?!"

Will startled awake at the thundering bellow. Vision still blurred from sleep. Will swallowed, his mouth dry and sour. Dread—cold and unforgiving—coated his lungs. Breathing became a chore.

"Holy crap!" Stella said, also awake.

"You asshole," Cam growled through his teeth.

"Whoa! Whoa! Cam!" Will raised both his hands in surrender, jumping over Stella and shoving her to the farthest corner of the bed. "It's not what you think."

"Really?" Cam's gaze landed on the wings sticking out of Stella's closet and pointed. "Isn't that the costume the girl you left with wore on Halloween?"

Stepping forward, Cam grabbed the front of Will's shirt and pulled him out of the bed.

"That's my sister!" His eyes were wild.

"Cam, let me explain."

But Will wasn't given a chance. With brute strength, Cam shoved Will out of Stella's room and into the hallway. Will looked back. Stella sat frozen, clearly in shock. His heart lurched. He wanted to comfort her more than anything else.

"It's okay," Will managed to say before Cam dragged him off.

"What is going on here, Camron?" their mother asked, face pale. She'd clearly heard Cam's outburst and had come to investigate.

"Nothing, *Nanay*, just taking out the trash," Cam said. He only referred to his mother by the Filipino term when his temper had gone off the rails. The great menace in his tone sent chills down Will's back.

Hearing his best friend call him trash struck Will harder than any physical blow could have. He stumbled on the stairs. Cam didn't stop. He was a freight train. All Will could do was try to keep up.

At the bottom of the stairs, Cam headed straight for the door and yanked it open. The entire time he kept one hand on Will's shirt, his grip like a vice. With a great heave, Cam threw Will forward. Will barely kept his balance as he staggered away.

"Get out of here!" Cam said. "And don't come back. If I ever see you near my sister again, I'll make you wish you were never born!"

Stumbling away from his former best friend, Will couldn't

wrap his mind around how quickly everything had gone wrong. All he wanted was to turn back and confront his friend. But Will also knew Cam. There was no talking to him in a temper. And part of him couldn't stop hearing the word *trash* echoing through his mind again and again. So, knowing he left his heart behind with Stella, Will took the coward's way out and left.

ONCE THE SHOCK of waking up to her brother going berserk on his best friend in some misguided attempt to protect her honor wore off, Stella scrambled out of bed. She raced past her mom, who said something as Stella passed, but she was too focused on stopping Cam from murdering Will on her behalf to pay attention.

Tearing out of the house, she found Cam standing on the lawn, breathing hard, fists at his sides. No Will. Stella breathed a sigh of relief. She'd been worried she'd find her boyfriend sprawled on the ground, bloody. Surely Cam hadn't had time to do too much damage. He loved Will like a brother and would have regretted hurting him. Then her anger sparked.

"What were you thinking?" she screamed at him, not caring if the neighbors heard. She was too angry.

Cam turned around and faced her. "I should be asking you that question."

"Nothing happened!"

"You were in bed together."

"And nothing happened!" Stella pulled at her hair. "You're the worst!"

"Why Will? You've got to be kidding me."

"Why not?"

"He's my best friend."

"Exactly! You should trust him."

"Of all the guys, Stella! Why him?"

"I like him."

Cam's face darkened. "Like all the other guys?"

"This is different." She hated how petulant she sounded, but her truth needed to be heard. "Will is perfect. I've liked him forever."

"Don't tell me that. He's not as perfect as you think."

To Stella, it felt like they were having two different conversations. "Why? Because he's your friend?"

"You don't understand!" Cam's eyes grew wide. "I know him better than you. He's a player. I've seen him in action. He hooks up with girls faster than a fisherman catches fish."

Stella pushed away the image of Will and any other girl. He wasn't like that. Not with her.

"You sound like a total jerk," she accused. "Ratting on Will? To what end? To turn me off? Well, all it proves is you were never his friend."

"Low blow." Cam actually looked hurt.

"And dragging him out of the house wasn't?"

"He deserved it! You're never seeing him again. Do you understand?"

"Who's stopping me?"

"Do you understand me?" The coldness of Cam's tone was final.

Stella sucked in a breath, trying to hold back the tears that flooded her eyes.

Cam softened his expression. "I'm just trying to—"

"Protect me." Stella choked out a laugh. "Yeah, sure. Tell yourself that."

"Stella . . ."

"No! You don't get to control my life." She shook her head, backing away. "I will like who I want, and you have no say in it."

"We'll see about that."

She put her foot down. "I can't take this anymore. I'm done."

With all the dignity she could muster, Stella squared her shoulders and stomped back into the house. She managed to hold back the flood of tears until she shut the door to her room.

SEVENTEEN
BREAKUPS ARE HARD

Will sat at his desk, waiting for Cam to get back from spring break. Six days might have been enough to cool his friend down so they could talk rationally about this. Will had driven back to UCLA a day early to make sure he beat Cam to school and that all baseball equipment and other paraphernalia that were possibly hazardous to Will's health—pens, books, shoes—were safely tucked away and out of immediate reach.

Will's feet bounced in anticipation. He rested his elbows on his knees and clasped his hands together. His big speech was ready. The key was to get Cam to listen. Will believed if he could accomplish that, then Cam would see reason. He believed his friend wanted Stella's happiness. Will needed Cam to see that all he wanted was to make Stella happy.

He jumped to his feet the second the door opened. Cam burst into the room with a box in his hands, not sparing Will a glance. He marched straight to the closet and shoved clothes inside without caring if everything wrinkled.

"What are you doing?" Will blurted out, his speech forgotten.

"What does it look like?"

"Let's talk about this."

Dropping the box, Cam rounded on Will and grabbed him by his shirt collar. Then he shoved him up against a wall. Will might have been taller, but Cam had superior upper-body strength.

"You wanna talk?" Cam growled into Will's face. "Let's talk."

Will gritted his teeth through the pain of his head banging on the wall. He didn't resist. Instead, he kept his hands at his sides and looked Cam in the eye.

"I love her."

"Wrong answer."

A fist came flying by to land on the wall by Will's head. Cam still had some sort of restraint. But the message was clear in the damnation in his eyes.

"How long?"

It was a question, but from Cam it sounded more like a threat. Will shoved aside all his insecurities about being with Stella. He wasn't running away this time. He was owning his feelings for her in front of the guy he loved as a brother.

"We became official the night of the Halloween party."

Cam's face paled. "God! I thought you were leaving the party to hook up. You were lying to me all this time!"

"Nothing happened. Then or when you caught us in bed together. I respect her too much to pressure her into anything she's not ready for. Please, Cam, you have to understand." Will swallowed. "Stella is important to me. I would never dream of hurting her."

"But she's like a sister to you."

Will shook his head. "She was never like that to me. She was annoying at first. Then she was this geeky girl with braids, braces, and glasses. Then . . . she was more."

His friend's face soured. "Are you telling me you've liked her for longer? Is that why you were in on chasing all those idiots away?"

"Since we were juniors. And yes. I was afraid that if I didn't help, then she'd find someone and I'd lose my chance."

"She was a sophomore," Cam said with disgust. "You're sick!"

"I never did anything about it," Will promised.

"Is that supposed to make me feel better?" Cam backed away. "And when you suggested you be her date to homecoming?"

"Don't ever think that I wanted to deceive you in any way."

"You were lying to me. All this time." Cam shoved his fingers through his hair. His expression went from enraged to betrayed. "But you know what was worse? That I counted on you to back me up. At the holiday party. You promised nothing was going to happen. I trusted you. You were my bro. You broke that. All because you thought to sneak around my back with my sister."

"I love her, Cam. You have to believe me." Every breath Will inhaled felt like needles in his lungs. "And I know she loves me too."

"Like hell that's true." Cam raised his fist again. Will braced for the blow. It never came. Instead, Cam pointed at him and said, "You and me, we're done."

Cam picked up the box full of his stuff.

"Wait!" Will reached out. "Don't do this. Please."

"You know all those guys that I thought weren't good for her?" he asked, pausing by the door. Will waited with bated breath. Cam turned and faced him, a stone-cold expression on his face. "You are worse than all of them combined."

Will staggered back as if Cam really had hit him. "Why? Why am I not enough? All I want is for her to be happy!"

"All of those hookups," Cam said, voice going eerily calm. "You used all those girls as what? Replacements for my sister?"

"Of course not. Damn it, Cam! Is that how low you think I am?"

"Yes." Cam opened the door. "That's why you're not worthy of her."

More than hurt by Cam's condemnation, Will snapped, "I don't think even Jesus himself would be worthy of her to you."

"I'm done talking," Cam spat at Will. "And I better not see you around my sister, or the punches I'm holding back will land."

The sound of the door closing rang out in Will. When Stella had asked him if he was prepared, his answer had been all wrong. He'd had no idea losing his friend would be so devastating.

The small dorm room felt infinitely emptier as Will sank to the floor and leaned back against the wall. Maybe he really was not good enough. He couldn't even get Cam to stop and listen to him, much less believe how he felt. He cradled his head in his hands. Maybe it was better to let Stella go. For her own good.

EIGHTEEN

FASHION ON THE BRAIN

Stella hadn't known she could cry and sew at the same time. She cried for Will and her broken heart. She cried for herself and her dreams that hung in the balance. And she cried for her brother. She hated him. Oh, how she hated him. But he was still her brother. Family. And that meant she still loved him.

Not that she was speaking to him. Oh no! Despite her mother's guilt trips, she still wasn't speaking to him.

The only bright spot in Stella's life came from the fact that her dress was done. The massive thing took up most of her room.

All the beads had been sewn on. All with the tireless help of Franklin. She couldn't have done it without him.

As if her thoughts had called to him, a knock sounded at her door. Tears still streaming down her face, she turned and sniffed. Franklin, eyebrow raised, handed her a tissue.

She took the tissue gratefully and blew into it. "What do you think?"

"I can't believe you're still crying" was Franklin's clipped response while he studied the dress.

His words triggered more tears, but tired of crying and eyes sore, Stella inhaled the biggest breath her lungs could hold. Then she exhaled it slowly. It helped settle her. A bit.

"Cut me some slack." She shifted. "Will hasn't been answering any of my texts. I'm icing my brother out. And I need this dress perfect before the model fitting tomorrow."

"Pain is really working for you."

"You think?" She tilted her head, studying the dress. "I can't see the taffeta for the chiffon anymore."

Franklin snorted. "You got that right."

"What's that supposed to mean?" Her hackles rose. Her eyes were suddenly very dry.

"The skirt is magnificent and the corset is on point." He cradled his elbow in one hand. "And you know how I love teal, but—and I mean this with love—are you sure about the sleeves?"

Stella's defenses magnified. "What about the sleeves?"

Franklin rubbed the fabric between his fingers. "They

remind me of a bad eighties prom dress. You already have the exposed shoulders. The fluffy drop sleeve is way too much."

The rubber band of her patience snapped. "You know what? I'm not going to take this from you right now."

Incredulous, Franklin said, "What? Some constructive criticism?"

"The dress is good. There's nothing wrong with it."

"But it's not great *yet*."

"Thank you for your help, but I think you should go. Focus on your own dress. You don't see me giving you 'constructive criticism.'" Stella sandwiched her last words in air quotes.

Franklin's face turned a bright shade of red that clashed with his hair completely. "Actually, I'd welcome the input if you ever bothered to ask about my dress. Here I am helping you, and not once have you asked if I needed any help."

"Well, excuse me for not caring while my life is slowly imploding." Stella threw her hands up in the air. "I'm not the one who got into Parsons."

"That's the problem." Franklin pointed at her. "It's always been about you, you, you. It's the Stella show twenty-four seven around here. You'll fit right in on *Project Runway*."

"I'm supportive!"

"What does my dress look like? What materials did I use?"

Stella opened her mouth to respond, but her mind drew a blank. She crossed her arms instead.

"See!" Franklin slapped his sides. "Not even famous yet, and already you're forgetting who your friends are."

"Don't be such a diva!"

He gasped. "How dare you!"

She pointed at the door. "Leave!"

"I will!" He turned and stomped away, but when he reached the door, he stopped and said over his shoulder, "Congratulations. Your life really has imploded."

"We'll see about that," Stella challenged. "My dress will kick your dress's ass."

When Franklin sighed, his once-confident shoulders slumped. "Yeah. Whatever helps you sleep at night." Then he walked out, head held high.

A part of Stella had regretted her words as soon as they'd left her mouth. Franklin didn't deserve what she'd said. But— and it was a big *but*—she'd show him. The sleeves looked damn good, and the votes from the crowd would prove she was right.

With renewed determination, Stella dabbed at her cheeks. Her focus needed to be on finishing the hand-painted roses she had planned as accessories. She could worry about Will and what was left of their relationship after she'd won the competition.

THE NIGHT BEFORE the competition, Stella sat in front of her sewing machine, making the adjustments. Her model was bustier than she had previously accounted for. She was so tired. Her eyes kept losing focus, so she kept blinking them. She developed a crick in her neck from hunching over so much. But she had to keep going.

She glanced at her bed as she fed fabric through the machine. Her sheets called to her. She resisted the urge to lie down. She could sleep after she'd won. The whirring of the machine didn't help. It was too hypnotic. Too consistent.

"Are you ever going to talk to me?" Cam said from behind her.

The jolt of surprise from her brother's sudden appearance woke Stella up like a triple shot of espresso. She breathed through her frantically beating heart. Then she lifted her foot off the pedal to keep from accidentally ruining the dress.

"Not until you stop being a jerk and let me live my life," she said, breaking her no-speaking-to-Cam policy. With Franklin deserting her in her hour of need and the continued radio silence from Will, Stella had a few things to get off her chest.

"Come on, Stella. I'm just looking out for you. You don't know guys—"

She dropped the corset of the dress, cutting him off with, "How am I supposed to learn if you don't let me?"

"Don't be that way."

Fed up, Stella pushed away from her machine and faced her brother. "Like what, exactly? Someone genuinely pissed off because you're keeping me from the guy I've liked since I was a kid? You throwing that same guy out of the house because he happens to feel the same way about me?" She pointed at him, causing Cam to shut his mouth before he could rebut her claims. "And don't even say that Will is like other guys. You and I both know he's not."

"I wasn't going to." He pushed away from the doorframe he

had been leaning on and stuffed his hands into the pockets of his cargo shorts. "I just don't want you to get hurt."

"You think Will is capable of hurting me?" Stella asked incredulously.

Cam stayed silent. As he should.

"Okay." She breathed hard and ran her fingers through her hair. The oily strands reminded her she needed a shower. "Are you saying you're really willing to give up a shot at the majors for the sake of protecting me? Because that's exactly what needs to happen when I go to college. There's no protecting me if you're not with me all the time."

Her brother finally dropped his gaze. A muscle jumped on his jaw. Stella could see the internal war he was fighting caused by the truth in her words. If this was the only chance she got to knock some sense into him, then by God she was taking it.

"Before Dad died, he made me promise to protect you and *Nanay*," he said.

Stella's face softened at the mention of their father. "That you did. In fact, you did such a great job that I couldn't experience life anymore. Do you think that was what Dad wanted when he asked you to take care of us when he couldn't?"

His shoulders came up. "I might have overdone it. A little."

"Ya think?"

She approached him and touched his bicep. He met her gaze. Confusion and protectiveness was evident in his hazel eyes. She went with a gentler tone when she spoke again.

"Cam, I spent most of senior year standing on my own two feet. Sure, some things didn't go my way, but I got up, dusted myself off, and kept moving." For the most part, anyway. But Cam didn't need all the details. "I can take care of myself."

"That's what I'm afraid of." There was a definite gruffness in his voice that she hadn't heard before. It was like he was trying his best not to be overcome by his emotions.

Stella smiled. "I appreciate you looking out for me. I really do."

"Then—"

She shook her head, cutting him off. "You have to allow me to find my own strength, Cam. I won't learn from my mistakes if you keep shielding me from them. Getting hurt sucks, but how will I find out how to deal if you don't let me go?"

"But . . ." The rest of what he wanted to say trailed off.

"But," she continued for him, "if I do find myself broken-hearted, I give you permission to hunt the guy down."

"Promise?"

"I expect nothing less." And she meant it too. That was, if she and Will still had a chance. But she feared that it was too late.

She pushed the thought away, not allowing herself to get distracted from what was important in that moment. There was no point in thinking of a future with Will if Cam didn't understand what she needed.

Cam cleared his throat. The tip of his nose grew red. Stella's heart melted. She wrapped her arms around her brother's shoulders, pulling him into a hug. In seconds, Cam was returning the hug.

"When did you grow up, little sis?" he asked as he held her at arm's length.

Her spring of tears welled up. "Being away from you does that."

"Ha-ha." He rubbed the heel of his hand against his eye. "If you tell anyone about this . . ."

"My lips are sealed." She giggled, blinking back tears.

"Do I want to know what that's about?" He pointed at the bracket.

Stella stepped in the way, hopefully blocking his view of the board. "Let me shield you from that."

He took a deep breath and nodded. "Fine."

"Now get out of here." She turned him around and nudged him out of the door. "I need to finish this dress for the show tomorrow."

Cam let her push him out into the hallway, but before she could shut her door, he said, "Are we good?"

She smiled again. "Yeah."

Then she closed the door. For the first time in a long while, Stella felt her shoulders lighten. A load lifted off them. She allowed herself a moment to sigh in relief. It really seemed like Cam understood what she wanted. But it still felt good knowing he was there when she needed him.

Done basking in her small victory, Stella put her game face back on. If there was ever a time she needed to push through, this was it. Imagining Tim Gunn giving her encouragement, she strode back to her sewing machine.

NINETEEN

LIFE IS A CATWALK, BABY

After getting a couple hours' sleep, Stella packed everything into her car and drove to UCLA as the sun came up. Thinking she would arrive early, she was surprised to see the makeshift backstage area of the Ackerman Grand Ballroom was already teaming with activity. Models were in hair and makeup, production staff were running to complete one task or the other, and designers were putting final touches on their garments.

Stella found her designated area. Beside her name was the Polaroid of her model in the dress. Once the garment was out of its box, she proceeded to the hair-and-makeup station and instructed the stylist on what to do with all the hand-painted roses she'd brought along as accessories. When she returned to her station, two assistants appeared as if by magic.

Just then it finally hit Stella. Her first real fashion show. Soon her creation would walk the raised runway she had passed on the way backstage. She inhaled the acrid scent of hair spray permeating the air. It was real. The first step to her dreams coming true.

She gave quick instructions. The assistants hopped to it. Steaming the dress. Preparing the rest of the roses that would go around the model's neck and arms like a floral chain. It gave her dress the over-the-top avant-garde push. Stella's model joined them twenty minutes before the show started. She wore a crown of teal roses on her head.

Stella didn't bother scoping out the competition. She had this in the bag. Although, once in a while, she'd look out for Franklin. She missed her best friend terribly. She promised herself she'd make up with him after she won.

WILL BARELY LEFT the dorm after Cam moved out. He knew in his heart that nothing would feel right with Stella if Cam hated them both in the process. The last thing Will wanted was to drive a wedge between siblings. But he also knew that he needed Stella in his life, despite Cam's feelings on the matter.

He needed to fix things with Cam. He didn't know how exactly yet. He hoped once he was done with the comic he was creating, the answer would come to him. He'd been working on the comic every day, even ditching class just so he could finish.

He was so engrossed with inking the final pages that he didn't notice the door had opened and closed behind him. Cam's empty bed beside him squeaked. He took his eyes off the comic for a second.

"Did you come to finish the job?" he asked Cam, who sat forward until his arms rested on his knees. Equal parts joy and fear coursed through his veins. "If so, can it wait? I just need to finish this."

Cam said, "I'm not here to punch you."

"Oh, good," Will replied, allowing himself a breath of relief. Then he waited. No matter how much he wanted to speak. To apologize. To beg for his forgiveness the way Nana had taught him. He waited. He knew Cam well enough to know that his friend did nothing without reason. If he'd come back to the dorms to see Will, then there was something he wanted to say. In the meantime, he continued with his inking.

"I talked to Stella," Cam finally said.

Will lifted the pen for a moment, debating if he should stop, but decided he had to finish, so he continued working. "And?"

Cam sighed. "She said I need to understand that I can't always be there to protect her. That she needs to learn what it feels like to be brokenhearted."

"I would never—"

"Stella is my sister." Cam sat up straight. "I will always feel protective of her."

"That's understandable."

Cam growled in annoyance. Will zipped his lips and threw away the key. Cam shook his head. Will knew it wasn't the time to be silly, so he nodded for his friend to continue.

"Stella actually gave me permission to hunt you down if you ever hurt her."

Will kept his mouth shut.

A long beat of silence followed Cam's statement. Will didn't doubt the truth of it for one second. Cam's gaze seemed far away. As if he was thinking. Will filled out the final word bubble on the last page of the comic.

"But if there was a guy who I trust will keep her happy, I suppose that's you," Cam said. He turned to face Will fully.

Will did the same, maintaining eye contact as he spoke. "I wasn't kidding when I told you I love her. I don't know how it happened. To tell you the truth, she's the one who has the power to break my heart, not the other way around."

Cam grimaced. "I don't remember you being this mushy before. Stella do that to you?"

Wiggling his eyebrows, Will added, "And so much more."

"Ugh!" Cam slapped a hand down his face. "Stop! That's my sister you're talking about."

Will grew serious. "Real talk?"

"What?"

"That's what Stella and I say when we're about to say something important."

Cam rolled his eyes. "You two are so gross." Will stared his friend down until Cam was forced to nod. "Fine. Real talk."

"I'm sorry for not telling you," Will said.

"Nothing would have happened if you did. I would have shut you down like a drug mule going through TSA." Cam pointed at him. "Just keep the PDA to a minimum when I'm around. And if I hear even a whisper of Stella unhappy, I'm coming after you with my bat wrapped in barbwire named Lucille."

"A *Walking Dead* reference. You are serious." Will pressed his lips together and reached out a hand. "Deal."

Cam looked from Will to his hand, then back again before taking it. But instead of a handshake, Cam pulled him into a back-slapping hug. Will went willingly, feeling a weight slide off his chest.

"Does this mean we're good?" Will asked when they pulled apart.

"Yeah." Cam grinned. "We're good. Now, what the hell are you working on?"

"It's a comic." Will handed the newly finished book he'd stapled himself to Cam, who flipped through it. "Oh, by the way, I think you should also know, in the interest of being honest, that I created a popular online comic with a character based on Stella. Vertigo is publishing it."

"Jesus H. Christ!" Cam buried his face in his hands. "How far does the deception go?"

Will retrieved the comic he had made before Cam could crumple it in a fit of rage. It was the only copy, and Stella needed to see it. "That's the last one, I promise."

"I didn't have to know about that." Then Cam took a deep breath. "No. I promised I'd be cool. You made a comic about her, fine. It's getting published. Good for you."

"Wow!" Will's eyebrows rose. "She really did it. She really put the fear of God into you."

"Shut up!" Cam screwed up his face. He stood from the bed and walked to the door. "Now come on. We better make an appearance at that show. She needs our moral support."

Tucking the comic into the back pocket of his jeans, Will stood from his desk and left the dorm with the biggest smile. His cheeks actually hurt.

STELLA WOUND A length of thread around her finger as she watched other dresses walk the runway on the monitor provided backstage, anxiously waiting her turn. A producer came to her workstation and gave her the five-minute warning. As one, Stella and the producer guided her statuesque model to the line of other models waiting to walk.

All eyes were on her dress. Pride mixed with fear in her chest. Doubt crept in at the last second. What if Franklin had been right? What if the sleeves were all wrong? She had been grieving. She hadn't been thinking straight. Hence the fight. Usually she listened to him.

"Breathe," she told herself, closing her eyes and imagining Tim Gunn standing right beside her the way he did with all the finalists when their collections walked on *Project Runway*.

The line inched closer to the opening that led to the runway. Stella made eye contact with her model. She winked at Stella. A quiet calm spread over her as her dress rounded the corner and disappeared.

Immediately, she shifted her eyes to the large monitor. Seconds later her dress walked out. The full skirt moved despite the layers and layers of tulle and chiffon. The crystals caught the light and glinted like stars in a teal sky. The corset gave the model a waist, and the sleeves that had worried her were the right touch, giving the dress an old-world feel. Fantasy come to life.

Stella brought her clasped hands to her chest. Tears stung the corners of her eyes. Her nose grew stuffy. Her dream. The dream of every budding designer. Watching her dress walk the runway. It had come true. She pinched herself just to make sure she was awake.

The camera moved with the model and caught two knuckle-heads cheering enthusiastically. Beavis and Butt-Head back together again. Her brother was whooping while clapping his hands. At his side was Will. He'd come. Will was there, with his fingers in his mouth, whistling so loudly she could hear it all the way from where she stood. The tears she was holding back rolled down her cheeks, but unlike the ones she'd been crying for the past week, these were hopeful.

Applause followed the exit of her dress. Stella saw nothing else as her model returned to her side. The tall woman leaned down and kissed both Stella's cheeks. The words "They loved it" were whispered into her ear. All the blood in her body seemed to rush to her head. It was too much. The emotions. The sensations. The idea that she'd just achieved something.

Almost numb, Stella worked on autopilot, helping the model back to her workstation. All models had to stay in the dresses until the winner was announced. She fanned her own hot face with a piece of paper. It wasn't enough to cool her down.

Gasps and exclamations caught her attention. Actually, everyone backstage was watching the monitors. A massive black dress—more like an architectural piece—walked the runway.

The skirt was made of studded leather. A giant wire-frame ball formed one shoulder. Spikes stuck out of the other shoulder. The makeup was black and fierce. The hair was styled into a spire on top of the model's head. The bodice was a cage of some type of wire; Stella's best guess was corrugated. She had used some once for an unconventional challenge with . . .

"Franklin," she breathed out.

It was his dress walking the runway, and everyone was enamored with its beauty. It combined savagery and grace. The very definition of avant-garde. It was the future of fashion.

Stella found herself moving to the front of the backstage area. Her eyes spotted Franklin's neon-streaked hair. She stopped to stand by his side.

Without taking her eyes off the screen—because how could she when something so beautiful walked?—she clasped Franklin's hand in hers and said with the deepest sincerity, "You're going to win."

"You think so?" asked her friend, voice shaking.

Stella gathered him into her arms. He fell into her embrace and held on tight. Soon her shoulder grew damp. She held on tighter and whispered into his ear.

"I'm so sorry for being so self-centered. It was unfair just to be thinking of myself. I should have been there for you."

"You were going through stuff," Franklin said against her shoulder.

"That doesn't excuse the fact that I wasn't there for you. Forgive me?"

Franklin pushed back to look her in the eye. "There's nothing to forgive."

Stella ran her thumb beneath his eye, catching one last tear. "Fashion should change minds. Do you remember who said that?"

"Duh. I did." Franklin's face crumpled like he was about to cry again.

She turned him around and pointed at the monitor. At his dress about to exit the runway. "That just changed people's minds. You're going to win."

"What about you?"

She shrugged, feeling weightless for the first time in weeks. "I'll figure something out. I always do."

She wrapped her arms around Franklin and hugged him to her as his model joined them.

"That's one hell of a dress," Stella said.

TWENTY

AND THE WINNER IS . . .

Not only did Franklin win, but he won by a landslide. Stella came in second. Not bad for her first competition. She vowed to try harder next time.

Clutching her certificate and the $1,000 cash prize that came with it, she pushed through the adoring crowd praising and taking pictures with Franklin and his chic creation. Both the model and her best friend soaked up the attention like sponges.

When Stella reached the front of the crowd, Franklin's face lit up. He engulfed her into a tight hug. Stella loved the fact that all was right between them.

"Looks like you have a couple of supporters of your own," Franklin said above the excited chatter.

He turned her around to face Cam. Will trailed a couple of steps behind her brother. Her heart was already beating really fast from all the excitement, but the second Will got within a few feet of her, it was as if her heart were trying to find a way out of her chest. Toward him, she knew. But she stopped herself.

Cam went straight to her with a proud smile on his face. "Congrats, little sis!" He pulled her into a hug.

She gratefully accepted the congratulations, but still said, "You know Franklin was the one who won, right?"

Not losing his smile, Cam reached out and shook Franklin's hand. "Congrats, bro. Well played. You beat my fashion nerd of a sister fair and square."

"Thanks, bro," Franklin imitated in a SoCal accent, shaking Cam's hand.

"Hey!" Stella smacked her brother's arm playfully. "Says the guy gaga over baseball. What do you know about fashion?"

"I know how to sew a hem," he said. Then, as if hearing what he'd just said, he grimaced. "Gah, you're infecting me."

"Good!" Stella and Franklin said at the same time, before they all laughed.

Then, placing his hands on her shoulders, Cam turned Stella toward Will. He had been patiently waiting on the sidelines.

"There's someone who really wants to talk to you," Cam whispered into her ear before nudging her toward a blushing Will.

Heart finding its way to her throat, Stella faced Will fully and took the last steps that led her to stand before him. She searched his face. His great gray eyes. The bump on his nose. The scar below his lip that she simply adored. All of it, she knew by heart.

"Here," he said, handing her folded pieces of paper.

"What's this?" She accepted it to find out they weren't just folded pieces of paper. They were stapled together to form a comic book.

"Just read it."

"Okay . . ." Unsure, she flipped through the pages.

It was another special side story of *The Adventures of Morla the Witch Hunter*. Like the one for Christmas. In this one, Morla was in jeans and a light sweater.

Jeans and a sweater? Stella's eyebrow arched. In fact, the clothes looked familiar until Stella recognized herself, not Morla. She was talking to a boy. Will. Her heart thumped. They were in the tree house. Will was holding her hands.

The real Will waited patiently as she reached the final page and the last speech bubble. In it was a question. It woke the butterflies in Stella's stomach. She covered her mouth with both hands after it had fallen open in shock.

The bubble asked: *The world deserves to know that I love you. Will you be my girlfriend again?*

She pointed at the comic. "Are you serious?"

Panic colored Will's expression, but he nodded anyway. "Please forgive me."

"What?" It was her turn to be confused.

"For being MIA."

Now both Stella's eyebrows went up, up, and away. "And here I was about to find you."

"To find me? Why?" Will's curiosity was genuine. It was like he'd never expected her to do such a thing.

"You're so dumb." Stella rubbed her eyes, easing the throb there; then she locked gazes with the clearly waiting-at-the-edge-of-his-seat Will. She gave in to his puppy dog face. "I was going to look for you because I thought, to hell with Cam. I want you, and I know you want me too."

"Oh, I want you." Will grabbed Stella by the waist and pulled her closer. "You were going to ignore Cam for me?"

"I was going to choose you, yes."

"Really?"

Will was so overcome with awe that Stella almost laughed. "Why is it so hard to believe?"

"You're too good for me."

"Are we back to that?"

"I had this whole surprise planned, and now we're here and you're beautiful and I missed you."

Stella stood back, concern creasing her brow. "What would you have done if Cam hadn't given in?"

The question seemed silly in light of the fact that they were finally free to be together. No more hiding. No more secrets. But she needed to know. Needed to see what he would have done.

Will's face grew serious. "Real talk?"

She swallowed, unsure at first, but she nodded eventually. She held her breath.

He sighed. His shoulders dropped. "To be honest, I didn't know what to do."

A horrid feeling settled in Stella's gut. He wouldn't have done anything? He couldn't be just like all the other guys her brother had scared off. Right? But as she feared the worst, Will continued speaking.

"I was happy you got through to Cam." He ran his fingers through his hair. "You were right. I wasn't ready to lose him. But you are important to me like nothing else." Then he met her gaze, his expression so sincere. "All I know is losing you hurt me more. I would have found a way. And I hoped that one day Cam would forgive me. You have to believe in that. Believe in me."

All at once, the twisting inside her cleared. She did believe him. In him. All this time she thought being with him was too good to be true. But this wasn't a dream. Will was real. And he was willing to fight for her.

Overwhelmed, Stella held him tight. "I believe you."

After a minute, Will held Stella at arm's length. "You haven't answered my question yet."

"What question . . . Oh!" She waved the comic and he nodded. The biggest smile she could muster spread across her face. "Yes! Yes! Yes!"

She jumped in place. In his arms. Where she always wanted to be. When she stilled, Will cupped her cheek and brought his lips to hers. The kiss was sweet. It was gentle. It was a homecoming.

"Eww! Gross!" came Cam's words from behind them.

Still smiling, Stella continued the kiss because it would take more than her brother's mortification to stop her.

WILL WATCHED IN awe as Stella handed the key of her hatch-back to Cam, asking him to drive her car and the dress back to Oak Hills. For a hot second, Will thought Cam would give them grief, but the most he did was give Will side-eye before he left.

"He's really going to be chill about this, isn't he?" Will asked, still not believing everything that had happened that day. He'd gotten his best friend and his girl back. And it wasn't even Christmas. He put his arm around her shoulders.

Stella snuggled closer to him. "I think he's trying."

They walked side by side around campus. Once in a while Will still caught himself checking if the coast was clear. Then he had to remind himself that it was. Cam had given his blessing.

"So," Will eventually said as they neared the dorms. "How does it feel winning second place? Congratulations, by the way."

She let out a long breath, then smiled. He couldn't get enough of that smile.

"Pretty good, actually. Franklin deserved winning first place."

"But the scholarship."

Her shoulders came up in a gentle shrug. "I still haven't heard from the other schools, so I'll wait before I figure out what I'll do next. It's not the end of the world."

"Whoa!" Will stopped and faced Stella. "What happened to the girl who pretty much thought she had no future because Parsons rejected her?"

She sighed, contented. "Let me see. I won a grand. I got you back. I got to see my dress walk the runway. So I'd say my life is pretty good right now."

He arched an eyebrow. "Getting me back is second to winning money?"

"Money I can spend. You I cannot."

"Oh, really?" He flipped Stella over his shoulder into a fireman's carry.

She squealed and flailed. "Put me down!"

"Not until you admit I'm better than money."

Laughter bubbled out of her, free and clear. "Never!"

SLEEPING IN WILL'S ARMS—just sleep—felt like coming home after a long trip. Welcome and necessary. She woke up knowing everything was as it should be. And when he smiled as he opened his eyes, her heart grew several sizes.

After eating breakfast at his favorite deli, he and Stella drove back to Oak Hills. They held hands for the entire car ride. Stella hid her smile in the palm of her other hand while her elbow rested against the truck's open window ledge. They didn't have to hide their relationship anymore. Her heart was full to the brim.

They arrived at her house at around lunchtime. Will opened her door for her. She expected him to leave for Nana's house, but instead he entwined their fingers together. Like a real, honest-to-God couple, they walked toward her front door. Will squeezed her hand as she opened the lock with her keys.

"Mom!" she called as they entered.

"They are back!" her mother said from the kitchen. In seconds, all four feet eight inches of the Filipino woman descended upon the both of them. "Did you make good time on the road? When Cam told me you were spending the night at his dorm I was worried, but he said William will behave, so I felt better." She nodded sagely, trusting her son's word implicitly. "But next time call first. You are grounded until graduation."

"Mom," Stella breathed out. Why was she still so nervous? Forget the fact that it completely slipped her mind to tell her mom about the sleepover. Now she owed Cam. She hadn't been grounded in a long time. Not the best situation to be in, but she'd deal.

"Yes?" Her mother looked toward her expectantly.

"This is Will," she said, gesturing to Will, who sucked his lips into his mouth as if he were trying not to laugh. She wanted to kick him.

Her mother's eyebrows came together. "Of course I know this is William. I do not have Alzheimer's yet. What is the matter with you, Stella Marie?"

"Mom." She cleared her throat. "I mean this is Will, and he's my boyfriend."

"Well, you're holding hands, aren't you?" She gestured at their clasped hands. "Then he is your boyfriend."

Stella rolled her eyes.

"It's good to see you again, Mrs. Patterson." Will stepped forward, as cool as a cucumber, and gave her mother a hug. Not letting go of Stella's hand the entire time.

"No, no," her mother said, taking his face in her hands. "You call me *Tita* from now on."

Both Stella's eyebrows went up. The honorific was a clear sign that she approved of Will being her boyfriend. "Wow, Mom, really?"

"Of course! We are family here." She gestured for them to follow her. "You come and help me set the table. We will have lunch. I cooked *sinigang*."

Well, it was indeed a celebration. The sour soup flavored with tamarind paste was Stella's favorite. She especially loved it with large prawns. Her mouth watered in anticipation. But first . . .

"Can I go and shower?" Stella asked.

"Go! William will help me," her mother said. "Come, William."

Will gave Stella a kiss on the cheek before he followed her mother to the kitchen. It was so surreal. The guy who was once Cam's best friend entered her house now as her boyfriend. After a minute of just standing there in awe, Stella climbed the steps. When she finally made it up to her room, she leaned against her doorframe and savored the happiness she felt inside. What more could she ask for?

She pushed away from the threshold. Fatigue from the days of little sleep and the aftereffects of an adrenaline high draped over her body like a heavy winter coat. Her gaze landed on her bed as she moved toward it. On the duvet was a large envelope.

A new burst of energy coursed through her. She jumped onto the bed and hugged the college acceptance letter to her chest.

Once she was sure it was real, she pulled out her phone and sent Franklin a text that said: *FIDM, baby!*

THE BOYFRIEND BRACKET
BREAKDOWN

TOMMY LARRABEE

* Captain of the debate team.
* Student council president.
* Passionate about Black Lives Matter.
* Activist.
* Articulate and charming.
* Won the election on his smile alone.
* Has political aspirations.
* Wants to be a lawyer.

★ ★ ★ ★ ♥ ♥ ♥ ♥

Give Tommy another chance.

He's a nice guy. Passionate.

KEVIN MARQUEZ

* Photographer at the school paper.
* Also works on the yearbook.
* Captain of the chess club.
* All he does is take pictures and talk about ultimate finishing moves in chess.
* Runs the school Instagram account.

★ ★ ★ ★ ♥ ♥ ♥ ♥

Cute, but too self-involved.

Totally no connection.

DANIEL CONNORS

* Captain of the swimming team.
* Talks about nothing but working out.
* Dreams of winning Nationals.
* Arrogant.
* Typical jock.
* Does not know when to take no for an answer.

Pervert.

JOEY ESPOSITO

* Running back for the football team.
* Funny.
* Cute.
* Confident. Knows what he wants.
* Straight A student.
* Has a high chance of getting a
football scholarship.

I like him.

→

MIKE CORTEZ

* Point guard for the basketball team.
* Aka Mr. Muscles.
* Looks like a thug but is actually very sweet.
* Opens doors and walks on the street side
  of the sidewalk.
* Plans to go to Duke University.

The Mr. Nice guy.

ERIC RICHARDS

* Plays the clarinet in band.
* Has sweaty hands.
* Cosplays as Mike from Stranger Things.
* Into D&D.
* Has freckles that run across his
  cheeks and nose.

Remember to watch Stranger Things.

AARON ANDERSON

* An artist.
* A brooding guy.
* Lead guitar in a band.
* Walks around with a rock-star vibe.
* Writes songs about each of the girls he has dated.
* Thinks he might be famous one day.

Too Taylor Swift.

HECTOR VILLEGAS

* Part of the glee club.
* Referred to as the Bruno Mars of the school.
* Great dancer.
* Is bi.
* Great dresser.
* Has aspirations of being an actor.

Reminder: Text Will. :)

Oh, pick up buttons.

ACKNOWLEDGMENTS

WHEN I BEGAN my journey as a writer, I always knew that one day the character that represented my roots would eventually make herself known to me. Little did I know at the time that it would take ten published novels and countless failed drafts that will never see the light of day before she would knock on my door. But when she finally came, she was fully formed and ready to tell her story.

Stella Marie Patterson would not have come to life without the help of so many people. Each and every one an inspiration and a source of comfort during this often solitary writing process.

First, I would like to thank my mother for epitomizing what a Filipina is. She is strong. She is resilient. She is a wonderful mother. A woman who puts her family above all else—even herself sometimes. She is patience personified. She is kindness. She is beauty and grace. She is a Filipina through and through.

Second, I would like to thank my editor, Holly. Thank you for entrusting me with the big brother's best friend trope. The moment you gave me this starting point, the book was born. I knew right away what would happen. I had no doubts. I wasn't afraid. I knew what to do. Your unfailing patience and support lift my writing to better heights. Thank you for making the editing process something worth looking forward to. And thank you for loving Franklin as much as I do. And for wanting to read Morla's adventures IRL.

Thank you to Eleonore for the wonderful, detailed notes. I would not have found my way in the dark without them. Thank you for being a part of the process and helping prepare this book for the real world.

Special thanks goes to Emily S., the Twitterverse, and FB for answering all my questions. So many dances. So many dates to keep track of. Your responses helped me build not only the town of Oak Hills, but also the high school where all the quirky characters interact. You are all a godsend.

I would also like to thank Liz D. and Emily O. for providing another excellent batch of covers for voting. I love each and every one of them. You helped give this book a beautiful face.

This acknowledgments section would not be complete if I didn't thank Swoon Reads. HQ built a beautiful community of readers and authors that support each other. Each new book that is released gets better and better. I'm always excited to grab a copy and read the finished product. Thank you for allowing me to be a part of this amazing family.

Thank you to my Grade 11 Creative Writing students of SY 2016–2017: AA, Bea, Janna, Marika, Kiyo, Cyd, Maia, Mickee, Nicole, Kosche, and Doty. You ladies inspire me. All of you make up some part of Stella. Fiery. Opinionated. Talented. Ambitious. And, most of all, drop-dead gorgeous inside and out. No joke. You were a pleasure to teach. Thank you for giving me the honor of being your teacher.

Thank you to Ms. Gerg for giving me a call. I wouldn't have considered returning to teaching without it. Thank you also for the friendship and the support. Our conversations in your office always make my day.

Thank you to Ms. Leah for welcoming me back into the fold and helping me regain my teaching legs. Your strength and leadership inspires me to be better. Do better. Putting me back in a classroom and entrusting me with students brought me back to life. So, thank you.

Thank you as well to Sister Adela for entrusting me with the creative minds of St. Scholastica's College–Westgrove. It is so great to be a part of an institution that fosters well-rounded students who are the future leaders of tomorrow.

Ate Loyce and Kuya Noel, you helped me stand during a turbulent time. I honestly would not have made it without you. Thank you for staying positive and always reminding me that I could do it.

And to the newest crop of Grade 11 Creative Writing students: Alyssa, AJ, Ericka, Nicole, Billie, Pam, Celine, and Robin. It's such a joy teaching you. Watching you grow and learn is worth getting up really early in the morning for. You eight know how to get things done. The next book is for you and your unfailing belief in love.

To the reader of this book, thank you for sharing this love letter to my roots with me. There is no one way to grow up. There is no one way to describe one's experiences. We are all human and it is in our humanity that we find what sets us apart from the rest. I hope that you enjoyed Stella and Will's story. It was a pleasure to write. Go forth and eat adobo. You never know who you might fall in love with.

FEELING BOOKISH?

Turn the page for some

Swoonworthy **EXTRAS**

REUNITED AND
IT FEELS SO GOOD

Stella bumped into the infamous Boyfriend Bracket on her way to the mirror. She caught it just in time and settled it back onto its easel. She didn't have the heart to throw it away. It might live on forever. A reminder of what she was willing to do during her senior year of high school.

With a smile, she gave herself one last outfit and makeup check. Her hair was pinned in an elegant swoop. She kept her makeup understated, but when she turned her head, the light caught wisps of glitter on her cheekbones. The real star of the show was the dress. It was a mermaid gown of shimmering gold with a sweetheart neckline. It was Franklin's gift to her, which he had decided to give to her early since her birthday was still a couple weeks away. He had been secretly working on it. No wonder he had commanded her not to think of making a dress. Thank God she'd listened because the gown was gorgeous. She was excited to see Will's expression when she came down the stairs.

Speaking of Will, he was waiting for her. If someone had told her this was what her life would be at the beginning of senior year, she would have laughed in that person's face. FIDM in the fall. The defeat of the Salads. Seeing her dress walk the runway. And, best of all, the name William Montgomery and the word *boyfriend* could be spoken in the same sentence. It felt like a dream she never wanted to wake up from.

A knock on her door pulled Stella away from her thoughts.

"Stella, are you—oh! You look like a movie star," her mother exclaimed. Her voice was filled with awe.

She turned to face her mother and saw tears in her eyes, which made Stella well up too. "Oh, Mom, you're going to make me cry."

"I'm a genius!" Franklin announced as he walked into her room, arms outstretched. Stella took his hands in hers. "It fits like a glove. You're a vision!"

"I couldn't have done better," she said, honoring his talent.

"Oh, I think you can. I know it." He smiled. His tux was in a bright electric green, and he wore a Keroppi pin in his hair. His boutonniere was an extravagant orchid that ate up most of his lapel. So like Franklin. His date knew him well.

Finally recovering from her shock at seeing Stella, her mother came closer and took Stella's hands from Franklin. Her best friend stepped aside.

"Oh, honey, you look like Sofía Vergara," her mother said, voice thick with emotion. "I wish your father could have seen you in this dress."

"Mom." Tears blurred Stella's vision.

"He . . ." Her mother swallowed, squeezing Stella's hands. "He would have been so proud of you."

Franklin was ready with tissues for the both of them. "Dab, ladies. Dab. We don't want to smudge the makeup."

Her mother dabbed away her tears and said, "I'll tell Camron to prepare the camera. You will come down soon? William is waiting."

Stella nodded.

"We'll just touch up her makeup," Franklin said.

Smiling, her mother left them alone. Stella finished drying her cheeks. Franklin picked up a makeup brush and pressed powder. With sure strokes, he refreshed Stella's face.

"The dress—"

"Is the least I can do for your eighteenth birthday," he said, interrupting her gratitude. "I know you'll come up with something equally amazing for my birthday."

"I will," she promised, not only to him but to herself as well.

After he finished with her makeup, he extended the crook of his arm to her. "Shall we? Our dates are waiting."

Stella wrapped her arm around Franklin's and as one they strode out of her room.

ON THE COUCH beside Franklin's date, Will bounced his leg while waiting for Stella to come down. Tita—it was oddly nice to call Stella's mother that because apparently it was a big deal in the Philippines—had already come down and said Stella was on her way. That brought him immense comfort because he hadn't seen her all day.

"Why you so nervous, bro?" Cam asked. "You're not planning anything with my sister tonight, are you?" Will lifted his gaze to his friend and waited. Eventually Cam shook his head and said, "I know, it's none of my business."

Will wanted to laugh. From time to time Cam's protectiveness still surfaced. He and Stella had learned to wait the reaction out until Cam came to his senses and backed off. Sometimes they even intentionally goaded him into being protective just for fun. Poor guy always took the teasing like a champ.

"They are here," Tita said. "Camron, come, bring the camera!"

"You mean your cellphone?" he asked. "I got it."

"I want a shot of them coming down the stairs," she instructed from the bottom of the steps.

Will pushed off the couch and checked the envelope that he had tucked into his inside jacket pocket. Still there. His heart jumped around in his chest. He hoped he hadn't gone overboard with his present.

Distracted by his thoughts, Will didn't realize he had reached the stairs until he looked up to a sight that took his breath away. It was like seeing the sunrise for the first time. His heart stopped. Her shoulders were bare. Her hair was up.

The dress hugged every curve of her body. She looked like a golden statue. How lucky was he that she loved him? The poor shmuck who once thought he would take his secret to the grave. Nana had been right to tell him Pappy's story. If he hadn't had the courage to tell her how he felt then, he wouldn't be standing exactly where he was in that moment.

The second they locked eyes, Will saw the future. It was of the two of them. Happy. Healthy. And loving each other for the rest of their lives. He was going to marry this girl, he thought as she descended the last of the steps and reached out for him.

The second she was at his side, he whispered into her ear, "Morla has nothing on you."

Apparently, it was the right thing to say because her blush was captivating. "You mean it?"

"Sometimes I wake up and still can't believe you're with me," he said as they posed in front of the mantel in the living room. Stella's mom barked instructions at them. He stood behind her and wrapped his arms around her until their hands entwined at her front. He gave her shoulder a quick kiss.

"Too close, bro! Ease up," Cam said, taking the picture.

Will and Stella smiled. Everyone waited.

Cam sighed. "That's fine. Sorry."

Stella let out a small giggle, and Will hid his chuckle by turning his head away.

"Now let's have all four of you together," Tita said, indicating Franklin and his date join Stella and Will.

For a few more minutes everyone endured the photo session. Then Franklin announced that they had to go if they wanted to make it to the gym before voting started. Stella and her mother shared a hug while everyone else filed out. Will took Stella's hand and tugged her to a stop before she too left the living room.

"What is it?" she asked, looking back toward him when they were finally alone together.

Again his breath caught. It was like every time he blinked he was seeing another side of her. Then he remembered why he had stopped her.

"I finally figured out what I wanted to do with my advance," he said, referring to the initial payment he had received for *The Adventures of Morla the Witch Hunter*.

"Oh yeah?" Stella waited, her face open and relaxed. She didn't suspect a thing. He pulled out the envelope and handed it to her. "What is it?"

"Take a look."

"It's not another scavenger hunt, is it? Because I'm not wearing the right shoes for one." She opened the flap and pulled out a piece of paper. She unfolded it. With each line she read, her eyes grew wider and wider until they couldn't go any wider anymore.

"A trip to the Philippines?" Awe was clear in Stella's tone.

"For two." When Will smiled his entire face lit up. "Think of it as an early graduation-slash-birthday present. We leave as soon as summer starts. What do you say?"

A couple of seconds passed. It seemed as if Stella couldn't believe what she was holding. She had mentioned the plan in passing, and Will had made it come true.

Once the shock wore off, excitement poured out of her. With glee, she jumped into his arms.

"Yes! Yes! Yes!" she said over and over and over again, peppering Will's face with kisses.

He laughed, accepting the kisses with relish. "At first I thought it was too much."

She hugged the itinerary to her chest. "It's perfect."

"What are you two still doing in here?" Cam asked by the front door, exasperated. "The limo is leaving without you!" Then he walked out again.

It was a joke, of course, because Franklin would never think of leaving them. Probably.

Not sure of the right answer, Will placed a hand on Stella's lower back, guiding her forward, the envelope and its contents still in her hands. He took such pleasure in making her happy. It was what he wanted to do for the rest of his life, not achieving fame or fortune. If Stella was happy, then his job was done.

Then the thought occurred to him, "Are you ready to win prom queen?"

She looked up at him as they approached the limo. "Not going to happen. No one is voting for me."

"With me on your arm, it might. Franklin predicted it."

Her brow furrowed in that cute way he loved. "Can a guy who doesn't even go to Oak Hills High anymore win prom king?"

His grin held with it a dollop of mischief. "I guess we're about to find out."

A COFFEE DATE

between author Kate Evangelista
and her editor, Holly West

Holly West (HW): Will makes a webcomic, *The Adventures of Morla the Witch Hunter*, in the book. What real-life webcomics would you recommend?

Kate Evangelista (KE): Oh! There are so many. For those looking for something LGBT, *Boy Meets Boy* by K. Sandra Fuhr is an awesome one. I read it every afternoon after class in college. Another was *Your Wings Are Mine* by Aoi Hayashi, but I'm not sure you'll find it anymore. Don't know what happened to it. I loved that comic to bits. For a comprehensive list of amazing webcomics, visit the io9 section of gizmodo.com. They have an article titled "17 Fantastic Completed Webcomics to Binge-Read from Beginning to End" that features some really good ones.

HW: Stella's favorite milkshake is double chocolate. What's your favorite frozen treat?

KE: Ice cream. You can never go wrong with a pint of Ben & Jerry's Karamel Sutra Core. OMG! My mouth is watering just thinking about it. Best eaten when it's raining outside.

HW: Will is an amazing gift-giver. What's the best gift you've received?

KE: My father's watch. It's a vintage gold Rolex that's custom made. Has his initials on the band and everything. I was just borrowing it one day because I was going on a trip, and he gave it to me. I cherish that watch and wear it whenever I can. It brings me luck.

HW: What fictional characters would be in your bracket?

KE: Peeta from *The Hunger Games*. Edward from *Twilight* (totally not embarrassed by this admission). Jace from the Mortal Instruments series. The Joker from *Suicide Squad*. Deadpool. Dean from *Supernatural*. Daryl from *The Walking Dead*. And Logan from *Gilmore Girls*, just to round out the bracket.

HW: The "falling in love with my big brother's best friend" trope was the inspiration for this story. What are some of your favorite romance tropes?

KE: I'm currently obsessed with anything that involves royalty. I mean, come on. Who doesn't want to be swept off her feet by a dashing prince? Plus, I have this fantasy of being a long-lost princess from a little known European kingdom.

HW: You've been a Swoon author since 2014. How has your experience on the site changed?

KE: Nowadays, I offer covers to any submission that catches my eye. I believe all submissions need a great cover. It's definitely part of attracting readers. So if I see a submission that doesn't have a cover and I'm inspired by the blurb, I create a cover and contact the author. It's up to him or her to use the cover I made. I'm just happy to stay creative.

HW: What was your best fan interaction? What has been your weirdest fan interaction?

KE: My best always has to be tweets from readers who enjoyed my book. I don't think anyone reads my work until someone lets me know. *laughs* The weirdest will always have to be those asking for a sequel that will never happen. I never know how to answer those questions.

HW: Do you have any advice for aspiring writers?

KE: "If you don't write the book, then someone else will." There is a high probability of this. So get to work on that novel. Your story is valid. It's needed. And if you don't write it, you will walk into a bookstore one day to see your story on a shelf with someone else's name on it.

HW: How long does it normally take you to write a novel? What is your process?

KE: Nowadays? About a couple of months. Only because I've switched to writing by hand for my first draft. I've come to realize that when I write out the first draft by hand, I'm less anxious about the process. No doubts. Then when I start typing the story onto my laptop, I'm no longer in drafting mode. I edit as I type, so technically I'm already working on the second draft. Works for me.

HW: _The Boyfriend Bracket_ is a stand-alone novel versus the Dodge Cove trilogy, which was always intended to be a series. Is it a different experience writing a stand-alone versus a series?

KE: I think stand-alones are easier to write. You don't have to worry about continuing the storyline or recalling the characters. You can move on to the next book with a new set of characters. I think I'll stick to stand-alone novels for now.

HW: Franklin and Stella are very into fashion. What inspired you to dive into that world?

KE: I'm a huge fan of *Project Runway*. I've been watching the show from the beginning. I even watch the All Stars and Junior spin-offs of the series. I love watching a garment come together. Also, I love *Sex and the City*. Like Stella and Franklin, I watched that show and its movies for the fashion. Such beautiful clothing. Another show with great fashion? *Younger*.

HW: Music has helped you shape your books. Did any songs inform Stella and Will's relationship?

KE: This time around, I didn't have a set playlist. I put my saved tracks on shuffle and whatever song came on, I went with. If I need something more appropriate for a scene I'm writing, I usually keep pressing skip until the right song comes up.

DISCUSSION QUESTIONS

1. *The Boyfriend Bracket* explores being in love with a sibling's best friend. Faced with this scenario, how would you go about confessing your feelings? Or would you keep your feelings to yourself? Why?

2. How would you describe the two main characters, Stella and Will? How do the two differ from one another and how do their personality traits and interests complement each other?

3. How would you describe Cam's character? How do you feel about his protectiveness toward Stella? What would you do if you were in his shoes?

4. Will creates an online comic as a way to express his feelings for Stella. If you found out that someone you had feelings for created a comic starring you, how would you feel? Do you agree with Stella's reaction to finding out about the comic? Why or why not?

5. Franklin helps Stella find a boyfriend for her senior year by putting together the infamous Boyfriend Bracket. What are your thoughts on this method of choosing a guy?

6. Should Stella have stuck with the Boyfriend Bracket despite the opportunity to date Will? How should Stella have handled the situation?

7. How do Stella and Will change over the course of the novel?

8. Put yourself in Will's shoes. How would you have handled dating Stella? Would you have told Cam right away or would you have kept the relationship a secret? Why?

9. Now, put yourself in Stella's shoes. Faced with rejection, how would you have reacted?

10. What did you think of Stella's relationship with Cam? How would you handle a protective sibling? What's your advice to someone with a protective sibling?

Check out more books chosen for publication by readers like you.

   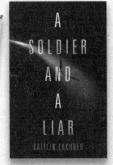

  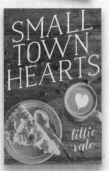